JOSHUA
AND THE
LIGHTNING
ROAD

Donna Galanti

To the real Joshua
who never fails to fill me with his own kid wonder and
adventure.

...and when the Olympian heirs at long last act with goodness in their hearts, an Oracle will arise to restore their full power and shut down the Lightning Road forevermore...

JOSHUA
AND THE
LIGHTNING
ROAD

Donna Galanti

Chapter One

I never knew lightning could zap you without burning you to a crisp. If it hadn't been storming something wicked that August day I never would have found out.

I looked for Finn out the window of my new room. We were supposed to work on our fort this morning, but the backyard was a muddy wasteland. The creek raced along like a roaring monster. We could go outside anyway, but that would never happen if my grandfather had a say. Bo Chez made me stay inside when it stormed like this. But even if we had to play indoors, Finn would save me from this boring day.

Thunder crashed overhead and lightning scorched the sky. My heartbeat ping-ponged in my ears, and my chest hurt. Dizziness overpowered me. I closed my eyes to make it go away. It always did.

When I opened my eyes, Finn was stomping in mud puddles as he made his way down the creek path. He looked like a giant bug with his backpack on underneath his black poncho. He was brave enough to wear a poncho. Not me. I worried about stuff like that. Like my gigantic clown feet. My stomach that poked out. The way my hair stuck up in back. Why Bo Chez had a magical crystal ball.

But Finn wasn't a worrier. He always made me feel better about stuff, especially when I freaked out over lightning like a baby. He didn't make fun of me. He just told me to think of it as nature's big movie, like my favorite tornado tracker show on the National Geographic channel. If I could choose a brother, he'd be it. We were like my favorite sandwich when we hung out: ham and cheese.

I ran out of my room, tripping over boxes still packed after two months. Why bother unpacking? It was just another new town and new school with new friends to be made. Maybe if I didn't unpack, we'd stay here forever. That was my other wish: to stop moving around.

I soon found out that was the wrong wish to make.

***

I raced downstairs just as Bo Chez yelled up "lunch!" and banged right into Finn sliding into the dining room. We laughed and sat down to eat. Traces of yummy warm toast filled the air, and my stomach rumbled as I dug into a Bo Chez lunch special: ham and cheese with a layer of sliced apples between two thick pieces of bread that oozed with mustard. It squished in my hands. The best crunchy sweetness ever, and I mumbled thanks to Bo Chez as he hovered over us.

"Tell us a story, Mr. Cooper?" Finn said through a mouthful.

"Yeah, a really good one, Bo Chez." I nodded.

"You're so lucky. He tells the best stories," Finn whispered to me. "And you get to live with him. My dad's just an accountant."

Bo Chez pulled his rocking chair closer to us and sank into it. The chair seemed to disappear as he took it over, which fit my name for him: Bo Chez. The Big Cheese. He even smelled a little like cheddar cheese mixed with peanut butter.

"What do you want to hear today, Finn?" Bo Chez tapped his thick fingers on the chair.

"Tell us about the Lost Storm Master," Finn said. Bo Chez nodded and spread out his hands, battling the air. Lightning splashed across his face and his gray hair stood up like tiny swords glittering under the chandelier light.

"The Lost Storm Master was a big barrel of a man with wild hair. He could create the fiercest of all lightning, tornadoes, and hail to defeat any creature or man." The room grew darker. Despite having heard this tale a dozen times, I shivered. "The Lost Storm Master was trained as part of an elite group of soldiers handpicked by the almighty Zeus, king of the Greek gods. These soldiers carried ancient magic in their blood."

Bo Chez paused for effect. The thunder outside sounded like it would split the roof open. Finn leaned in and the screen door banged with the wind as Bo Chez continued.

"When Zeus discovered the Storm Master's fondness for a young girl, Asteria, he banished him at once, for his soldiers were not allowed to love. Zeus didn't miss this Storm Master until the day a giant killer eagle descended upon the gods, terrorizing its citizens. It attacked with such speed and fury that no one could defeat it—not Zeus, not the other gods, and not even the entire army of Storm Masters. Zeus sent messengers to all corners of their world to find the Lost Storm Master and bring him back to save them. And he did."

As Bo Chez went on with the story, his special crystal glinted at me from the shelf above the fireplace. It was locked in a wood and glass case and the size of a giant jawbreaker, but a mix of clear and cloudy like a glass marble. Bo Chez had told me never to take it out. Light quivered across the crystal ball now, and it seemed to spin as if it contained a storm of its own.

Bo Chez got to the part when the evil eagle attacked again. "The Lost Storm Master flung his lightning orb so fast that the winged beast caught on fire mid-air. *Whoosh!* The murderous, flying devil perished in a fiery blast. Then the Lost Storm Master dragged the beast back to Zeus and cast it on a bonfire. All of the gods rejoiced, for they were saved."

Finn was right. My grandfather was definitely more interesting than an accountant.

Bo Chez stood and filled our view. "Boys, I have to run to the convenience store quick to get batteries and candles in case the power goes out. Will you be okay alone for twenty minutes?"

"How many times do I have to tell you I'm not a kid anymore?" I said. You would think turning twelve last week would have changed the way he treated me.

He raised an eyebrow. "Fine. I'm only a phone call away, and stay inside and don't touch anything you shouldn't."

"We won't," I said.

"Promise," Finn agreed.

"And stay away from the windows if it starts lightning again."

"*Okay.* We get it," I said.

Bo Chez backed his car out and reached the end of the driveway before reality sunk in. Finn and I were alone in a house full of things we weren't supposed to touch. The anxiety was almost too much, but we had the whole house to ourselves!

"Hey, Joshua, want to play hide-n-seek?" Finn said.

"Sure." He loved our big house for just this reason. Even if it was a kid's game, I went along with it for Finn's sake. "We'll pretend the house is haunted. Find me or the ghost gets you and turns you into one!"

"I'll count. You hide."

"Ham," I said.

"And cheese."

Finn grinned and his freckles got bigger. He punched me twice on the arm, and I punched him back. Our thing. Then he bolted upstairs.

I pretended to count on the way to my bedroom as Finn stomped up to the attic. "Seventy-five!"

Light flashed across my room, and then the power went out. I grabbed a flashlight from my dresser and headed out. Long shadows flickered around me, and lightning lit up the hallway. The wooden floor creaked beneath my feet as I tiptoed toward the attic door, sliding my fingers along the cool walls.

"One hundred. Ready or not here I come!" I said with more courage than I felt, pushing the attic door open.

Inky black swallowed me up. I darted my flashlight about, but its small, round light didn't reveal much. The mustiness of old things hidden away filled my nose. *Bo Chez, hurry home*. The hair prickled on my forearms as the stairs screeched with each step and the landing loomed in front of me. Could a ghost with an axe be waiting to chop off my head? I took a deep breath, waiting for a blade to fall, but the only thing lying in wait was a dusty bookshelf.

"Finn-man, I know you're up here." I flicked the flashlight around the room, its cold metal warming in my sweaty palm. Thunder crashed over my head and my ears popped.

One more step forward.

"Got ya!" Finn jumped up, his shadow against the

window. I tripped and landed hard on my butt. My flashlight twirled across the floor.

Then a blue arc of light struck the window. Glass exploded. Finn's mouth froze in a wide 'O'. I yelled and reached out to pull him down, but another zap of light blinded me. Finn screamed. Rain splattered my face, stinging with each drop. White dots floated in the air. Something gray billowed past me carrying a familiar, rotten stench that made me gag. A knobby hand grabbed me. I bit it and shoved it away, gagging again, and the hand dropped me back on the floor with the taste of salty dirt on my tongue. An angry howl blasted the air.

Zap. Zap.

Daggers of light shot everywhere as sharp glass cut into me.

"Finn!"

He floated in the shadows. Light erupted all around him, his eyes round with fear. The sky boomed overhead, and a deep laugh bellowed out as if the thunder itself were taunting me.

"Next time it's you, boy," a raspy voice said.

Wind shrieked around me in a ferocious wail, pulling me with it. I flattened myself on the floor and clung on tightly to the foot of a chair. The angry wind finally stopped. Rain pelted me through the broken window. All was quiet. I lifted my head.

Finn was gone.

Chapter Two

The rain continued to blow in. I stumbled to the window, crunching on broken glass, my legs weak. What if he was lying on the ground with a broken leg? Or worse. But a soft flash of lightning revealed nothing below.

I fumbled around until I found my flashlight and shined it about, searching for the owner of the hand that had grabbed me. Again, nothing—or no one—was here. Who *was* that man? Where had he taken Finn?

I had to do something, but what? I rushed back down the stairs to the living room. It was still dark in the house and my flashlight was dying. The thunder and lightning had stopped, but the steady rain continued to pound the roof. It grew louder in its attack as if trying to get in. Wind raced around me from the open window, and I shivered despite the muggy air that blew across me with the scent of fresh cut grass.

Bo Chez—I needed my grandfather. My trembling fingers punched in the number for his cell phone, but the phone line was dead. If only he had let me have a cell phone. I ran to the front window. The driveway was empty.

I ran to the kitchen and looked out back. The creek was a wall of mud and water, the path now washed away. I could push through the thick brush to Finn's house or take the long way around on the road to get his family's help, but how could I explain the weird thing that had happened in the attic? And what could they do? It struck me then how lucky Finn was. He had a whole family who would miss him. Only Bo Chez would miss me, and if I had a brother I would protect him, no matter what.

A lingering toast smell filled me up, reminding me of my aloneness. *Think!*

There was no time to wait for Bo Chez's help. What if the road had been washed out, too, and Bo Chez wasn't coming back soon? What if Finn was dead? Time ticked faster as my head reeled with so many questions.

My one terrifying choice: to try and get Finn back by myself. I took off to my room and, with no idea what could come in handy, snatched up mini chocolate bars and a pen flashlight, and crammed them in my pockets along with my favorite drawing pencil. Would the lightning come back and take me? It's not supposed to strike in the same place twice. But that scary voice told me it would, and it hadn't sounded like it was kidding.

Bo Chez's crystal! He said it had the power to command the very heavens. I just thought it was part of the stories he made up. He told me that I would know what the crystal's abilities were in time, but who knew when that would be? I needed power—needed to *believe* it had power—and I needed it now. I ran downstairs, pried open the case with scissors, and with shaking hands took the crystal. It pulsed through my fingers, then glowed blue and grew warm.

I gasped and almost dropped it when a shiny square of paper tucked inside the corner of the case in its seam caught my eye. I tugged it out to turn over a laminated photo and sucked in my breath. I had never seen a picture of my mother, but Bo Chez had described her so often it was like staring at the exact image I created in my head. I ran my fingers across the smooth surface of her face.

Bo Chez told me we lost all our photos in a fire when I was a baby. Why would he have kept this from me? My mom smiled at me with big, blue eyes and wavy hair, the same colored eyes and dirty blond hair as mine. Diana. Her name was Diana. She died just after I was born. I bugged Bo Chez for more stories about her, but he gave me only vague details, except one: my mother never told anyone who my father was, not even him.

I'd lived my life without a mother, but I needed her now. I shoved the photo and crystal into my pockets and ran back up to the attic.

Sweat ran down my back as the warm August air washed over me and the scent of earthworms filled my nose. Thunder rumbled far in the distance. I pushed aside the broken glass and knelt where Finn had stood. Water bled into my jeans from the rain pooled on the floor. It seemed like forever ago that I wished Finn would hurry up and get here.

Lightning flashed. I welcomed and feared it. My chest tightened, but there was no time for panic. The crystal warmed my fingers through the deep pocket of my jeans. Bo Chez had to be right—the crystal had powers. What would they be?

Thunder crackled.

"Yeah, just come and get me!" I yelled into the storm, and a bolt of light took the tree across the creek. The top exploded in a fiery ball, then sizzled black. Thunder broke loud over my head like a giant clapping his hands together, and blue light exploded through the broken window. Two rough hands yanked me up.

Light blazed everywhere and heavy, scratchy material bound me tight as I was pulled upward into a swirling wind tunnel.

Anger felt better than fear, so I kicked my kidnapper. "Where's Finn?"

"You'll find out soon, Reeker."

Daring a peek, I saw a wide gray hat slung low over one green eye that blazed at me. Where the other eye should have been was a crater. One side of his face oozed red, melted mush! The man from my nightmares!

"Finn!"

The man held me tighter, choking off my words. His stink made me want to throw up. I strained to see over his cloak, wondering where his smell had struck me before. It hurt to breathe, and dizziness engulfed me, knowing the monster in my dreams was real.

Yellow and white ribbons of fire snaked before us in a black tunnel, and I froze in absolute terror. Lights ricocheted through the darkness on either side of me like shooting stars. We moved faster and faster. Wind roared everywhere.

"Stop looking around!" The man in gray knocked me hard upside the head.

I sank into darkness.

Chapter Three

I came to just as I heard, "Enjoy your new home, Reeker."

My kidnapper had some nerve to say I stunk. He smelled like a wet dog that had been swimming in sour milk and burnt grease. And then I was flying through cold air as the man threw me. Out of the corner of my eye, figures dodged left and right to part the way for my landing. Fog and faces spun around me. My body slammed into something hard, and sharp pain flashed along my side as rock cut into my hands. Dirt filled my mouth, and I spit out slimy pebbles and sticks.

The faces around me became clearer as dozens of boys and girls crowded into me. A few stuck out their hands and pulled me up from the trampled ground of the dirt corral we were packed inside. Frantic, I swung around to find a way out, then saw the fence. It was made of wooden stakes lashed together with frayed rope. Each stake rose taller than any kid by a few feet, and at the top of each a metal spear tip glinted fierce, ready to pierce any who dared escape. Lanterns, hanging from poles surrounding the fence, glowed far too dim to see much of the forest that spread beyond. Trails of mist blew around us and threatened to choke me as I gulped the bitter tasting air, focusing on the ground to get my bearings.

Find the calm. You can do it. That's what Bo Chez told me when lightning freaked me out, and freaking out would not help me find Finn. I stared in disbelief at the pale purple twilight sky and dim blue sun that sagged over me, the washed out colors sealing me into this strange painting. This was nowhere near home. My lungs finally unfroze and my legs stopped shaking as I stomped my feet on the rocky ground to get warm.

The kids checked me out. Some looked me up and down and some just stared at me with wide eyes and inched away. They didn't seem to be a threat, and I had so many questions, but they silenced me with a collective shake of their heads. I rubbed the gravel off my hands, leaving behind stinging prick marks, and looked around my prison. The fence wound around us with no gate going in or out, and a giant platform as high as the stakes stood before us. The fence ended on either side of it, and on top of the platform sat a white-canopied tent with an open front, the flaps tied back like curtains. We had no such protection from the mist that breezed across my skin, covering me in a wet chill. The one way out of this prison was by two sets of stairs leading up to the platform on each side, and down the other side toward freedom. I considered making a run for it: up the steps, across the stage, down the steps, run fast into the woods. How far would I get, and to where?

"There's no way out, boy." My gray-cloaked kidnapper towered above me from the platform where he had thrown me. The angry-red side of his scarred face was partially hidden by his flopping hat, and under it, that one green eye burned into me just as it had in my nightmares when he'd tried to kill me with a lightning bolt. He tapped his thumbs on his fat stomach that spread under a dingy, white shirt, and his stubby legs were squeezed into black pants that clung to every bulge and rolled over the tops of his brown boots like a brim of blubber. He scratched his bumpy half-nose, snaking his eyebrow in concentration, then stuck a sausage finger up the good side of it and rooted around to pull out a green glob and flick it at me. It landed at my feet with a wet slap.

"That's the only food you'll get today, Reeker!" He laughed a deep, horrible laugh and then spit. A brown chunk plopped on my sneaker. "And there's your dessert. Now they'll put you to work with the rest of these Reekers."

"Not before I find my friend you stole." It burst out of me, sparked by a surge of courage.

The man jabbed the air at me with a crooked stick he pulled from under his cloak. My bite marks cut across his filthy hand. *Good*. His one eyebrow crinkled into a long, hairy snake as he scowled at me. The kids around me shrunk back, their sour sweat blowing over me as they moved, and beneath the smell of their fear lay the smell of rain and mud.

"Think you're here for a play date, boy? I could have been a soldier if it weren't for the likes of you Reekers. Now it's payback time." He tugged on the scraggly beard that flowed down his cloak, then spread out his hands. "Listen up, Reekers. You're going off to work soon and good riddance. And you'll work hard or you'll lead a much more miserable life than need be."

With that, he turned and swung his hefty, ugly self away from the platform, his gray cloak billowing behind him like a storm cloud. I heard a horse whinny and then the thundering of hooves. Probably the very horse on which he'd carted me from wherever we landed. There was no waking up from the nightmare this time. As soon as he left, the whispers began.

"I want to go home." "How long do we have to stay here?" "Do you think they'll let us go?" "What's gonna happen to us?" "I don't want to die."

Their words churned around me when a boy leaned down in to my face. "*Allo*, where'd you come from?" He had dark skin and a strange accent and smelled like the mothballs Bo Chez packed in our winter clothes. I shook the spit off my shoe and straightened, reaching into my pockets. My mother's photo and the crystal were still there. I gripped them tight, staring at the tall, skinny kid whose black hair sat plastered to his head. He tugged on the hem of his torn T-shirt to stretch it down, but it barely reached his waist, and his giant sneakers poked out from jeans that were way too short to be cool.

"New York." My dry throat made it hurt to talk.

"I'm from France. We're from all over." The other kids nodded, many with dirt-smudged faces streaked with tears. Small groups huddled here and there, but a few stood alone and just stared at the sky as if it could magically whisk them away. There were about fifty of them and most were my age, but where was Finn—or a way out?

Two men on the platform held giant spears with tips that waved like flags blowing in the wind. A trick of light in the fog? No—hissing snakeheads with yawning mouths revealed shiny fangs. The heads darted back and forth as forked tongues flickered in and out, searching for something to strike. One head focused on me, its jaws stretched open wide as if it could swallow me whole. It leaned forward on the spear that held it in place, and venomous foam dripped from its mouth. Its glittery eyes told me just how eager it was to sink those fangs into my neck.

I shivered in my T-shirt and looked away at the outline of trees stretching beyond the fence into the unknown darkness. A burnt electric smell charged the air as static burst from the hanging lights like bugs being zapped. The eerie sound made the cold and damp even worse. Fear of not finding Finn—and of dying—crawled through me like a diseased worm.

The sounds of so many kids crying made my own despair worse, and I turned back to the tall boy hunched over. "Where are we? And who's that guy in the cloak?" My voice must have gotten louder because he put his fingers to his lips.

"Shh. Don't want those guards over here."

I whispered this time, tapping my foot to calm my nerves. "Is this another country?"

He chewed on the skin around his fingernails and shook his head. "The Lost Realm of Nostos."

"Where?"

"Another world connected to … ah … *la foudre*."

Another world echoed inside me as I stumbled from my jittery tapping and twisted my foot. Pain shot through me, and the knowledge this wasn't Earth. He grabbed my arm to steady me. I pulled on my bangs, a safer alternative to foot tapping.

"La what?"

He took his finger out of his mouth and waved it as he struggled for words. "The guard called it the lightning … lightning road."

"What we came down?"

"*Oui.* A road of fire."

"It didn't burn."

His eyes scrunched up and the finger went back in his mouth. "I thought I'd died and was going to hell surfing those flames."

The wind whipped around my head like the fierce wind of the fire road. "Yeah, a scary space roller coaster. What happens if you fall off it?"

"I guess you die. You can't breathe in space." But we could breathe here, even with this foul, tart air coating my tongue. The boy scrunched further down. "Besides, where would you end up?"

"Somewhere better than here, and away from the gross man that took us. Who is he?"

The boy switched from finger chewing to knuckle chewing and leaned in closer. His bony arms and legs stuck out at angles, and he frowned his pointy face. "The Child Collector. Or one of them. He steals kids to sell them off here in the auction pit."

"He called me 'Reeker.'"

"*Oui*, they call us Reekers because they think we stink—*odeur infecte*. Ha!"

It would be great to infect that Child Collector with some nasty disease.

"I've dreamed about that guy."

"Have you been here before?"

"How could I?"

The boy shrugged, as puzzled as me, and the guards yelled at us to shut up. The low buzz in the pit quieted down.

I lowered my voice. "I've got to find my friend. Did you see him? He's got black hair with freckles."

"They just sold off some kids to the power mill before you came. Maybe he was one."

What kind of place sells kids?

Focusing on the tall kid took my mind off the awful mess I'd gotten myself into. He picked at his ripped black T-shirt with a faded skull on it and shuffled his worn sneakers. One had a big hole on the side.

"Why are you still here?" I said.

"Ahh, not sure." The kid banged on his skinny chest. "Too tall? I'm Charlie."

"Joshua."

I stuck my hands in my pockets to find my chocolate stash and split it with him, careful to hide it from the other kids. He nodded, grateful, and stuck it in his mouth. "Sweet *chocolat*." His big eyes widened then closed with happiness. Mine tasted like a piece of home. It melted, sweet on my tongue. Too soon it was gone.

"What do they want from us?" I said.

"They steal kids from Earth for their workhouses. Something about being slaves to the heirs of the gods."

"What gods?"

"No idea."

And to think I'd laughed at Bo Chez's adventure stories. If only he were here to tell me how to save Finn like the heroes in his stories. I was no hero.

Suddenly, the other kids crowded in closer and shoved Charlie up against me, their heat swelling across me in waves. And then I saw why.

Four black foxes had joined the guards on the platform and trotted around them in loops—except they were unlike any foxes that had run through our backyard. Their heads were even with the shoulders of the men and their legs were as big as a horse's. Fur covered them in slicked back, shiny spikes. They sniffed the platform and panted, thick tongues pulsing out of their mouths, and saliva dripped down in big gobs.

Muscles rippled up and down their bodies like quivering arrows as their bushy tails swished back and forth. I flinched with each swish, my feet desperate to run, but they were frozen in place. The foxes jerked their heads up in unison, and it felt like spiders skittered up my spine. Red eyes glowed bright like lava and burned fiercely into mine, hungry for what I feared was me.

"Cadmean beasts," Charlie whispered to me. The kids pushed us back, moving away from the monsters on the platform. I tripped, heading in the same direction, just as a big gust of wind almost knocked me over. Charlie grabbed my shoulder to keep me on my feet.

One of the guards stepped out from the tented canopy, lifted the top on a wooden chest, and hauled out a bloody slab of meat almost as big as the chest. He dumped it on the platform near us with a splat, and the foxes leapt at it, snarling and howling. Each pulled off a piece. They could just as easily lunge down into our pit and tear us apart, limb by limb. One of the beasts looked up from its feast and stared at me, coals of fire burning bright. Its ears twitched and juice dripped down its giant jaws.

And then it grinned at me.

My bones petrified right then and there, melding my body into one big, unmoving log. The beast went back to eating, savagely shaking its head back and forth as it ripped and shredded its dinner.

My toes curled under, wanting to hide.

And I knew: I was in over my head. Way over my head.

Chapter Four

I looked away from the monstrous foxes and strained to see beyond the fog, when a girl with bright orange hair tugged my shirt. She looked like a leprechaun with big green eyes and freckles like Finn's, so I decided to call her Red.

"You don't want to go to the power mill." Her accent was thicker than Charlie's, but different. She felt my arm up and down, and I pulled away from her. "Nice muscles though. You'd work out good there."

"What happens at the power mill?"

"That's where they send the boys. They need you to make light and energy," Red said. "They use us girls for different things on Nostos, and in other lands." She shook her hair angrily, and water drops sprayed us.

"Other lands? Like this one?"

Red nodded. "Some with deserts and oceans and volcanoes. At least, that's what I've put together listening to the guards since I've been here." She glanced around, then spoke quieter, her eyes growing bigger. "They say there are worse places than this. We could be digging in the coal mines on the Fire Realm. They traded a bunch of big boys yesterday to go work there for some fire god."

That awful reality hit hard, and I shared a scared glance with Charlie who gnawed at his knuckles again, now marked red across both hands. I didn't know if making energy sounded any better than digging coal mines. My throat burned with the thought, and I squeezed my elbows into my sides and changed the subject. "Doesn't the sun ever come out here?"

"Not a sun like ours," Red said, pointing at the pale blue sun hanging over us that faded in and out between the mist in the treetops. "And all it does here is mizzle. Like back home in Devon."

"Mizzle?" Charlie screwed up his face. "That's not a word."

"Is so," Red said.

"Is not," I said.

"Misty drizzle."

"So made up," Charlie said.

"So not. We're being mizzled on right now," Red said with a serious face.

"Better than being whizzled on." I swallowed a laugh that boiled in my throat, tasting the acrid air.

"Not funny. It's a true word from the English moors I come from. You saying my people are liars?" She looked like she would cry like so many others here, and I didn't think I could take that.

"No, no, *mon amie*," Charlie whispered for us both, and all joking disappeared. We were quiet as a guard paced the platform and cracked the air with his snake spear, threatening to zap us just for fun, then he retreated back under the canopy.

I pointed at Red. "How long you been here?"

"A week," Red said.

"In this pit?"

"No, they cart us off at night to a big bunkhouse where we sleep, then bring us back here." A tear squeezed out of her eye and rolled down her cheek.

"Has anyone escaped back home … or to other lands?" I said, after she wiped her face.

Charlie and Red looked at one another and back at me. I pushed my fingers against my forehead, waiting to hear good news as the crying kids, the laughing guards, and the crackling lights all throbbed inside me. I stared at the ground and kicked the dirt with my sneaker, pushing it away.

"One kid tried today," Red finally said and grabbed my arm, leaning in with sour breath. This time I didn't pull away; her fingers were like ice cubes pressing into me.

Charlie nodded.

They stood in silence until I couldn't take it anymore. "What happened?"

"He climbed the fence—" Charlie said.

"—took off running—"

More silence.

"The foxes held him down—"

"—while the vapes struck him," Red finished.

"Vapes?" I said.

"Vaporizers. The snake spears the guards carry," Red said. "They blasted him good."

"And just like that, he disappeared." Charlie nodded, chewing his bottom lip. "*Désastre.*"

Disaster and death.

"Oh, man," I said, holding my breath, not wanting to suck in the air filled with dead kid dust.

A bell rang and the guards stood up straighter.

"What's happening?" I looked over at Charlie. He stood up straight for the first time, his height giving him a clear view.

"The Auctioneer is back." He hunched down again.

A tall, thin man in a black gown with a hooked nose stepped up to the platform and the kids stopped whispering. Mist drops ran down my face and neck, and the breeze turned into icy prickles on my skin. Panic churned in my gut and exploded up my throat.

A small boy carrying a clipboard stepped up beside the Auctioneer. He was thin and pale with huge black eyes, white hair, and wore a gray shirt with black pants. The boy smiled at me. I smiled back, daring to believe someone here could help me.

The Auctioneer shuffled his papers and, muttering to himself, stepped under the canopy to scramble about a desk, searching for something. He yelled at the guards to help him look. The boy stood on the platform, waiting with his hands folded together and stared at his feet.

"Charlie," I whispered. "I've got to find my friend and get home."

He stared down at me, his eyes as blue as the sky back home on a sunny day.

"Just this morning I was reading to my little brother who was home sick," Charlie said. "My dad's always traveling and my mom had to go to work, so I stayed with him, but now he's all alone."

He sucked in shaky breaths. *Don't cry.* I would, if he did. I remembered a kid at my old school whose younger brother went missing. They never did find him. The family was all messed up about it. And then all those missing kid reports on TV ran through my head. Were they here? Doom filled every part of me.

"You're lucky," I said. "I don't have any brothers or sisters. Just a grandfather. Kids at school made fun of me for that."

He nodded and blew out a big breath of faint chocolate that smelled like the promise of home. "Well, I don't miss my dad. He's always yelling at me. Told me I'd never make any money wanting to be an artist."

"Hey, I want to be an artist too," I said, hoping to make him feel better.

"That's cool. Are you good?"

"Sometimes. Are you?"

"My brother thought so."

He poked his thumb into his cheek and looked like he would cry again.

"You'll get home," I said, wanting to believe it too.

But Charlie just shook his head and lowered his voice. "We're Reekers now. I'm not saying you won't find your friend. You might. But we'll never get home again."

To an only child who moved as much as we had, "home" had no great meaning. But now the word held everything lost—Bo Chez.

The Auctioneer huffed and, grabbing what he found, made his way back to us. I rubbed the crystal in my pocket, its smooth surface comforting me with the hope of power.

"Time for you Reekers to get to work. This auction is open for business!" The Auctioneer frowned down at us and banged his stick on the platform, then rang a bell with his long, misshapen fingers. It clanged across the auction pit as he grinned with jagged brown-spotted teeth.

Nothing about his smile made me think I would ever get home again.

Chapter Five

A fat, scowling chef bought plenty of girls for the bakehouse, and a skinny woman with gnarled fingers and black nails took a bunch of boys and girls to the greenhouse. Many went willingly, but a few struggled, crying and dragging their feet. The threat of being vaporized kept them moving. One soldier needed servants for the king and passed a bag of gold to the Auctioneer to buy several big boys.

Between patches of mist the purple sky rolled from lavender into violet, and the dim sun deepened its blue as time beat on. An orange moon slipped over the woods and rose in the sky. It seemed like I'd spend another day with Charlie in the corral, but at the last moment, a tall woman in a green-hooded robe walked closer to the edge of the platform. In one swift movement she pulled her hood off to fling back curly, black hair that streamed down to her waist. Her skin glowed pearly white and her blood-red lips stood out like ribbons on snow. I feared her beauty more than the Child Collector's hideous face. Beautiful people had more power than ugly ones.

"Come along, then," the Auctioneer prodded the woman. "Got some good strong ones here for power mill work. See any you like?"

Finn could be at the power mill! Having faced my fear of lightning to find my friend, something drove me on. I came here to rescue Finn, and there was no turning back. In trusting Charlie's words that Finn could be at the power mill, there was only one thing to do.

I shot up my hand. "I'll go."

The kids took in one giant breath and widened their circle around me as the Auctioneer raised both eyebrows and shook his stick at me. "A volunteer? Now that's a first. You Reekers really are dumb." The guards joined him in laughter and the cadmean beasts threw their snouts in the air, no doubt having fun at my stupidity too.

But the woman remained silent, staring at me with her head cocked and black eyes piercing mine.

"What are you doing?" Charlie tugged on my shirt, but I shook him off.

"I'm not staying here. I came to get my friend."

He let go of my shirt. "It's safer in the pit."

"Maybe, but there's no way out. There could be a way out somewhere else."

He didn't respond, and then his hand crept up too.

I shook my head at him, but he only raised his hand higher. We were partners now.

The woman's stare bounced back and forth from me to Charlie.

She flicked a long finger at both of us, claiming us as her power mill slaves, along with fifteen other boys, and then she disappeared like a ghost through the haze. Was she the energy god?

We were ordered to climb the steps, and in doing so found ourselves surrounded by guards on the platform. My new world grew bigger as I stood high above the comforting pit I'd chosen to leave. A dirt road wound away from us into the woods, taking with it the thrumming of horse hooves galloping away. The wind's fingers pushed and pulled at me as the kids below watched and waited.

Trees loomed around us, their splotchy birch bark glowing against the purple sky. Some twisted branches spiked upward while others sloped toward the ground and buried themselves in the earth as if hiding. I clenched my knees together to keep standing and watched the remaining sea of faces in the auction pit to focus on anything but where I might be going. There stood Red. She nodded at me, her face pinched, rapping her knuckles together. Back to the bunkhouse for her. Was she the lucky one, or us?

"Listen up, Reekers," the Auctioneer rasped out. "If you don't work hard, your new boss will send you back and I'll lose money—the Child Collector loses money." He dragged himself forward, his stick clack-

clacking on the wood floor. "And we never lose money. And if you *do* get sent back, you'll be cleaning out the castle sewers with the rats. And these aren't like Earth rats." He picked his teeth with a ragged nail, pulled out a mushy lump, and peered at it, as if considering its worth, then chomped on it in delight. "These rats are as big as cows with tails to whip you and teeth to gnaw your tender noses and fingers."

He laughed with a snort but had a coughing fit and had to stop, and then waved to the boy with the clipboard. "They're all yours." Standing close to him, the boy now looked older than me, maybe thirteen. He smiled at me again, but this time I had no smile to return.

The giant foxes snapped at us, rounding us into a tight circle. One of them brushed its thick tail against my leg, its enormous jaws level with my head. Razor-sharp teeth threatened to bite me in two, along with a mouth that could swallow me in one greedy gulp. The stink of raw meat blowing around me in the breeze made me choke on the throw up that rose in my throat. It burned going back down, and I pulled in my stomach, trying to make myself look less appetizing.

The Auctioneer and the clipboard boy took a step back. The kid mouthed something to me. *What did he say?* He mouthed it again. *It will be okay.* It sure didn't feel okay.

"Here they come," Charlie whispered in my ear.

A dark swarm swelled in the sky. Dozens of wings fluttered and a cool wind swept toward me in waves.

I rubbed the crystal in my pocket crazily, wishing hard to make the birds disappear. It didn't work.

"The korax," Charlie said in a cracked voice. "Hold on tight. I saw a kid fall just before you got here." He smiled to reassure me, although he nervously bounced a curled thumb to his mouth. "But he squirmed a lot. Screamed too. Broke his leg. They took him off to the bunkhouse doctor."

Charlie certainly had guts for wanting to come with me.

As the swarm drew closer, they appeared as monstrous black ravens with a giant wingspan that filled the sky's empty spaces. Their massive beaks opened and closed with gurgling croaks, but it was their eyes that terrified me. They burned a bright green, shooting us with a mean glare as they torpedoed down. Chanting words echoed across the dark land: *light bringers, light bringers.* Imagined words? The whirring of wing beats throbbed in my head as they grew closer, matching the beat of my own thudding heart.

The cackling screech of these mutant birds slammed through my ears as their beaks opened on giant hinges, and tongues like fat worms squirmed about in cavernous mouths. Screaming kids pushed up against me on all sides as a rancid wind roared over us. The words *light bringers* stabbed me over and over, and I cupped my hands to my ears. The other boys stampeded around me, shoving, yelling, but the guards pushed us back, vapes hissing. We had nowhere to go, not with monsters and men on all sides.

"Wh-what do I do?" I grabbed Charlie's arm.

He gripped my arm back—just as scared as me. "Well, don't squirm, that's for sure."

I nodded, terrified.

"And don't scream."

One of the korax swooped in. Giant talons clamped down hard on Charlie, and then he was gone. His long legs swayed up and away. Something nabbed my collar and pulled me off my feet. A scream stuck in my throat as I rose into the air. All around me screaming kids dangled from talons as long as my arm.

With every move of its wings, a stench, like something half-eaten, crawling with maggots and buzzing with flies, wafted over me. The puke in my throat threatened to come up again, but out of my side vision birds flew below me with their captives, and I sure didn't want to puke on anyone. We left the auction pit lights behind and flew into the dim nothing. Everywhere in front of me legs swung below feathered black blades that cut through the air in the misty gray.

We skimmed the tops of trees that stabbed upward as if to shred me with their fingers. Pointing my feet up away from them was the one movement I dared to make. If I startled this flying beast, it might drop me to be shish-kebabbed on giant toothpicks. I remained frozen, hoping this flight of terror took me to Finn. Old dreams of flying came to me, of floating out of my bedroom window and soaring over the woods back home. But not here. Not now. Not in this evil place that took my world away.

After a few minutes, a light glowed ahead. It grew larger and larger until it spread across an area as big as a football field. Power lines ran back and forth around a humongous brown building and fed into a big box on the roof. A fat, misshapen chimney hiccupped smoke that hovered in a thick cloud, and soft light gleamed from the building's windows. A faint *chooga-chooga* noise grew louder until it became almost deafening, a steady pounding over and over.

Chooga-chooga. Chooga-chooga.

The swarm dove down into this sound.

We had arrived at the power mill.

Chapter Six

My bird chauffeur dropped me to the ground, gave me a hard peck on my head in farewell, and jetted off. I was grateful to be back on land—and alive. The other kids fell around me, and we crammed together for warmth. Another tall fence, like the auction pit one, contained us, and we faced massive double doors that stood twice as tall as me. The entrance to the power mill.

My new prison stretched like an abandoned warehouse, never-ending in the dark. Fogged-up, broken windowpanes were scattered across the building like old mouths with missing teeth, eager to consume me. Bars clutched at the glass, twisted and bent, holding back whatever wanted to get out. The mill's wooden walls were singed, and a bottom floor had caved in, leaving burnt, blackened beams hanging lopsided, waiting to fall. The top of the building sagged like the mall rooftop back home that had been crushed under a Christmas snow. And over the doors were etched the words: *Bring light of life upon this land, for death awaits you in the resting. Toil on!*

Very soon I would know what that meant.

Chooga-chooga. Chooga-chooga.

Every *chooga* engulfed me with the loss of my world, my friend—and Bo Chez.

Charlie's black hair poked up above the group of miserable kids. I pushed my way through to him, choking on the dust dozens of anxious feet stirred up, and tapped him on the shoulder. He jerked around, but before he could say anything a new sound pierced the air. The double doors opened slowly with the painful cracking of old wood.

Yellow light flowed out and revealed the tall woman in the green robe who had bought us. She stood on a walkway overlooking us, more witch than god. Fog spun around her as the building sucked it inside. Her robe fell to just above the floor, an emerald quilt threaded with gold flecks that glinted in the light and shimmered like liquid. She strode toward us down the walkway as if floating and then stopped. All that shiny green swirled around her and fell still. Pointy black shoes with gold jewels peeked out from her robe and tapped the floor in an impatient rhythm. What crazy mess did I get Charlie and myself into?

Guards ran through the doors and surrounded us with vapes. The sound of kids screaming jolted me back a step, my own fear bursting inside me. The doors opened wider and revealed the *chooga-chooga* noise. What appeared like dozens of giant hamster wheels lined the floor behind the woman, and the floor above her, and the floor above that, all in an open warehouse. The wheels were made of curved wooden slats with spaces between them like big unfinished barrels, and all boys powered them.

"Joshua, how do they keep up?" Charlie whispered to me. "I can't do this."

"If *they* can, *we* can." It sounded braver than my insides felt, as guilt for leading Charlie here lurched through me.

"For how long?" He poked his tongue in his cheek over and over, nibbling on a thumb.

"As long as it takes to get out of here."

Finn wasn't the only kid in need of saving.

The woman smiled. Blue teeth filled her mouth like she'd just eaten blue candy, and she stretched out her arms, motioning for us to enter. "Come, my lovely new Reekers." Her voice rose over the noise. "You're miles from that cold auction pit. Don't be afraid of hard work, for it will warm you and power our land."

The guards forced us inside, and we had no choice but to move forward. The fence stood too high to scale, and beyond it spread a darkness that could hold creatures scarier than the ones we'd already seen, happy to peck out our eyeballs or gobble us up for dinner. The doors creaked shut, and with a final *boom* we were trapped.

Before me, hundreds of kids moved their legs back

and forth as flexible metal tubes connected to gloves on their hands threaded through the slat spaces in their hamster wheels and floor grates. The tubes spun upward, coiling together in one enormous braid, and from top to bottom they fell from floor to floor like streams of silver raining down.

Sad faces haunted me—faces that mothers and fathers missed, that grandfathers missed. Their faces had no emotion, no need to escape, as if they were already dead. I wanted to pull each and every kid off and yell, "Come on, let's go!" We'd take down the guards and use the vapes on them. *Zap. Zap.* But most likely we would be the ones to die.

Steam filled the room, mixed with the smell of sweat and moldy wood. A steady hum came from their work, and the *chooga-chooga* sound drummed inside me. The kids pushed into me from behind, and moving forward I could now see where the tubes from the workers' hands gathered near the ceiling and fed into an enormous yellow balloon that floated over us like a giant cracked sun. It hung ragged with brown patches on it as if it had been repaired many times. The balloon swelled and deflated, filling up with every beat of the monotonous *chooga-chooga* sound. Were the tubes feeding the kids something through their hands, like an IV, to make them work harder? The whole factory was a freaky, breathing thing.

A rectangular sign caught my eye. It had hooks, and each hook contained a red card with a number. A guard kept changing the cards, and the number grew bigger and bigger. At the corner of each floor, a guard paced alongside the kids, shouting insults and shoving vapes in their faces to make sure every single kid worked his hardest.

The boy with the clipboard stepped out from behind the woman. He wasn't smiling now.

A whistle rang through the air and a bell gonged. The thunderous noise of the power mill came to a sudden halt, and in its absence came the soft panting of hundreds of red-faced boys. Each hiss of a vape in the sudden quiet jolted into me like an electric current. The balloon deflated, and the number on the ticker now read one hundred. I scanned the kids from floor to floor, searching for Finn—and a way out—but saw neither, and stuck close to Charlie who was so hunched over now, his head bent down to his waist.

The woman clapped her hands, and the sound cut across the silence. "Bravo, my wee workers. Maximum output has been generated for the moment. Take a break. Get a drink and a bong bong to eat while I show our new friends to their places."

The kids limped off their machines on each floor and formed a line to a water and bathroom station. The guards prodded them with the blunt end of their snake spears, growling at them to keep moving. Another guard handed out biscuits from a bag to each kid as they passed him, and they crammed the snack in like they hadn't eaten in days. My stomach bubbled at the thought of food.

The woman clapped her hands again and addressed

our group. "Form two lines here so Sam can record your entry and ready you for your machine."

We did as she said and shuffled toward Sam. Charlie stood in front of me. My stomach gurgled louder, and I pressed my hand against it to shut it up. The woman stared down her tilted-up nose at us, raised her arms, and spoke.

"My name is Hekate, and I own you." She towered over us, black eyes ablaze with power. "And you now work for King Apollo. You will produce the energy our land needs to survive. This is your only worth, and you will be branded as slaves of the Lost Realm." She laughed at this while visions filled me of a flaming red iron brand being shoved into my skin. "You will work in eight-hour shifts and must make your energy quota for the day or there will be consequences."

She paused and looked at us one by one.

"You do not want to face those consequences, my adorable Reekers." Hekate folded her arms across her chest and paced up and down between our lines. Her emerald robe flowed behind her, and her shiny hair bounced as she glided back and forth. She took a step toward me, sniffed twice, and then tipped her head as if figuring out what she smelled. She finally shook her head and moved along. "When your shift is done you will be directed to the bunkhouse. There, you will eat and rest and be awakened to begin another eight-hour shift. Darlings"—she lifted her arms in a theatrical swish—"welcome to your new life."

The Child Collector strode in, and I gripped my

stomach harder. His jumbo belly pointed the way, and his cloak swayed behind him. Goosebumps rippled across my skin, remembering him gripping me tight under his cloak up against that gross body.

"Checking on my investments, Kat." His melted flesh stretched gruesomely across his face, and his one eye settled on me. He poked a beefy finger my way, and I wanted to claw the remaining eye right out of his socket. "Make sure this one works extra hard. He bites."

"No worries there, brother. He'll work harder than he's ever worked in his whole miserable Earth life, or else ... " She smiled at me, leaving me to wonder what that *or else* could be. The Child Collector leaned into me. He needed no words—his smell was threat enough as his stink washed over me. My left foot skittered back and forth on the floor, and my stomach erupted a horrible wail.

"Silence!" Hekate slashed her long finger at my face, and I considered extending my hobby as a biter. It would probably be the last bite I ever took. "Animals don't speak. They don't get fed, either, unless they behave."

She and the Child Collector moved away from me. "I smell something here I haven't smelled in a long while." I strained to hear Hekate speak to him, their heads bent together.

"It's not likely, Kat."

"Still ... I can't be sure of it beyond your stench, my dear."

"Ah, but that isn't me." He laughed. "That's the glorious smell of bacon beer."

She shook her head, black curls tumbling. "We must keep watchful. We can't have everything ruined. Zeus can't get wind of it."

"These Reekers are traded all over Nostos. If a special one existed it could be anywhere—or nowhere."

"Yes, but I've been stopped too many times by another. I'm old and worn out."

"You don't look it." He tugged on one of her curls. She gave him a soft laugh and waved him away with a hand while flouncing her robe. He cleared his throat and his voice grew deeper. "But this body of mine *is* worn out. Let me have a new one."

She darted her eyes to us and I stared straight ahead, holding my breath. "After our big day, Cronag, when I have time and can locate the rare plants I need to work such complex magic. You know it's been years since I've found them." He gripped her wrist and she didn't resist, but moved in closer to him and spoke so softly I had to strain to hear. "I'm sorry. I know it's not how you desire to look, but you're my handsome brother no matter the flesh you take on."

"I could have been a soldier in Ares's army if not for this one eye."

"I know, I know. But then I wouldn't have you as my best collector."

He let go of her wrist and tugged his hat down over the melted side of his face. "At least let me take down the one who did this ... " He stroked his scarred cheek and winced.

"In good time, you shall. We'll find him. I promise." She put a pale hand to his red face.

"If you make good on your promises, Kat."

"I always do."

The Child Collector grunted, then moved in closer to Hekate and whispered something I couldn't hear. She mouthed back one word: *Tomorrow*. He smiled grimly, then seized his cloak on either side and strode out the door.

The boy in line next to me started to cry. Nudging him didn't work. He only cried louder. Hekate stopped before him with her hands on her hips, so close that her thick scent of roses wafted over me.

"There is no escape," she said to the crying boy. "There is no return to Earth and your mommies and daddies. You are mine until you turn eighteen and head to the adult work camp." She burst out a shrill laugh, and I stood up straighter. The boy behind me continued to cry. *Stop, kid!*

"Silence, ignorant Barbaros!" Hekate snapped her fingers as if she could command this entire world. A guard came forward, his vape spear pointed at the boy. Poisonous goo dripped from its fangs, poised to strike. All the kids in the power mill stopped moving forward in their break line and turned to watch us as if they knew what headed our way. The guards watched as well.

"I don't want to vaporize you." She waved the

guard back. "You haven't worked off your cost yet. I need to sell the energy you'll make." She flung her long fingers out at the boy. Blue sparks shot out of them, and I stumbled back. She could make fire from her fingers!

"Out of sorrow, plays delight. Tears no more for your plight," she sang. "Make music galore. Tonight!"

I ducked, hoping it would save me from her sparks. The boy cried louder and then stopped. He stood with his mouth open as sad music floated out. His crying had become the melody from a tiny harp. It rolled around the power mill, echoing back.

"Aha! How wonderful." Hekate laughed again. "Your crying is now music to my ears. Cry on!"

The harp hypnotized me, tipping me into a dreamy state. I closed my eyes and floated away on it when a hand grabbed my arm, snapping me back to reality before I fell. Charlie gripped me. I blinked the tired waves away, drained of all hope that I'd ever find Finn and get us home.

Hekate clapped her hands again, making me jump. "Don't be frightened, my little Reekers. You'll be stronger in no time." Our owner then swept off through the power mill by another set of doors. Relief curled deep in the pit of my stomach that she and her fire-blaster fingers were gone.

Two guards stepped in to flank Sam as he motioned for us to move forward. He recorded each boy's name and stamped something on his arm. Thank god, not a brand of fire, just a mark. The harp music dwindled away as the kid next to me wore himself out.

I trudged forward behind Charlie, waiting for my brand. And my machine.

No longer did I belong to just me.

And in the silence that once held the *chooga-chooga*, I found myself chanting, *I'm Joshua. I'm Joshua.*

Chapter Seven

As I got to Sam, the break ended and the monster hamster wheels started up again. Hundreds of kids pumped their legs, heating up the power mill, and the scent of sour sweat and mildew snaked up my nose. Sam's pale skin and white hair reflected the yellow in the overhead lights. Up close, his shirt and pants fell baggy on him like hand-me-downs he'd never fit into, and his skinny arms poked out awkwardly from puffy sleeves that were too big. His face was round but had tiny features, as if he weren't all the way grown.

"Name?" He didn't look up from his clipboard.

"Joshua Cooper." He shook his head as if he didn't hear me, so I said my name again, louder. This kid had told me back at the auction pit that everything would be okay. Would he help me now?

I whispered in his ear, flicking a thumb at Charlie close by. "Help me and Charlie here get back home?"

A guard stepped forward with a scowl, leaning his vape into my face. I took a step back.

"Give me your arm," Sam said. He tilted his head toward me as if he wanted to say something, but instead he stamped my arm with the silver-dollar sized shape of a sun—only not a fiery one, a black one—and pushed me aside. "Next!"

All of us kids had the same brand and, looking closer, it appeared the circle that enclosed the sun included these words: *A noble cause you bear. Your fleeting sun lives on, cast in darkness. We breathe fire from your body, destined to lie in ashes.*

"Charlie, this is all my fault," I whispered to him as we both stared down at our brands that connected us now even more.

"What is?"

"Getting us here."

He looked at me with shiny eyes. "You said somewhere else could have a way out."

"Or someone," I said out of the corner of my mouth.

"I thought I was going to die in that pit until you showed up," Charlie said.

We're probably going to die here, I wanted to say.

Once we were all stamped, Sam led us past rows of hundreds of kids back at work. We climbed a set of stairs to the third floor, the wide-open grates making me dizzy. I slid my hand along the cool wood railing to steady my steps, afraid I would fall through, bounce off kids and wooden wheels like a giant pinball machine, and zoom toward the floor. *Splat.*

At every turn, guards with vapes watched over us. One grunted as I passed, punching the air with his spear in warning. Noise vibrated upward through the grates and flowed into me. Electrifying.

Chooga-chooga. Legs swung all around me. Back and forth. On and on. We marched by kid after kid who ran on rickety hamster wheels, gazing ahead. The harp music followed along behind me. That kid was crying again. *Chooga-chooga.* The balloon above swelled and deflated.

We soon reached an empty section of the third floor. Sam led us each to a machine. Mine happened to be a wheel right under the balloon. The tubes from all the wheels rose up through the grates, like the paths of worker bees feeding the Queen Mother, and hot tar fumes filled my nose like the smell of my driveway back home in summer.

Next to me, Charlie stared at the balloon. Did he imagine it like me growing bigger and bigger then *bang*? I flicked my eyes around the power mill for an escape: a door, a window without bars on it, stairs to the roof. There must be a way out! A guard jabbed me in the stomach with the blunt end of his vape and yelled at me to stop looking around. My eyes welled with tears as I clutched my burning stomach and stared at Sam. His eyes flitted over me, but then he begun instructing us on what to do when a guard yelled "Stop, Reeker!"

A boy ran past us screaming. Sparks shot up from around his feet as the guard's vape fired over and over.

The grates below my feet shook as the boy streaked by, scrambled up on his wheel, and began working furiously next to me. His thick hair bounced up and down with his efforts. It took all I had to remain still as stone.

The guard strolled over and said to Sam, "That one doesn't get his break until his shift is over."

Sam nodded. He moved toward the boy, who pumped his legs faster and faster. Sam bent down and pulled up a chain from the floor next to the wheel. At the end of it dangled a handcuff.

"No!" The boy jerked his hand away. In a second the guard was there with his vape inches from the boy's face, the snake's tongue flicking in and out. Charlie inched next to me, his hot breath beating down the back of my neck.

Sam grabbed the boy's hand and held it down, snapping the cuff on the boy's wrist. In that click, my own fate was locked.

"Please, Sam, don't," the boy whispered.

"You know the rules. Anyone late back from their break must pay the consequences."

"P-p-please. Hekate doesn't have to know."

"Silence!" The guard ordered the boy.

Zap. Zap.

Fire streaked through the air, curling my eyelashes and seizing me with terror. The boy screamed, and every muscle in me quivered. I held my breath and closed my eyes tight. When all was quiet I opened them, fearing the boy had exploded into dust. He still stood there, but his hair had been burned away. Smoke encircled his head. The guard laughed and laughed.

"One more word and I'll zap all of you, Reeker, not just that curly top of yours."

Sam turned toward us, a frown on his face. "Once a day in here you get food and five minutes every hour for water and a bathroom break. Five minutes. It's all Hekate allows." He sounded sorry about it, as if he wanted us to know he had nothing to do with that rule. "Everyone get on your wheel."

We all stood for a moment unmoving. The same guard menacingly strode toward us. "Now, you filthy Barbaros!"

The guard thrust his spear at us, his vape's tongue spitting sparks. Imagining myself vanishing into a million pieces of dust, I rushed up on my wheel. In front of me, metal mitts dangled from tubes that threaded through the open wheel slats, and Sam instructed us to put them on. We had no choice as the guard glared at us. The mitts' rough metal scratched and tugged at my fingers. These tubes weren't *giving* food to us. They were *taking* from us.

"Begin!" Sam raised his hands as a gong boomed.

I hurried to work my legs. Faster and faster I turned my wheel. It looped under me again and again, making me dizzy. Charlie ran like crazy on his wheel, barreling toward the same place as me: nowhere. Before long, blood beat in my ears, sweat trickled down my back, and my shirt clung to me. I was desperate for water, and my head throbbed with heat. My fingers felt like tiny bugs were crawling all over them, nibbling as little jolts stung me. The gloves sucked at my fingertips, pulling energy out of me and sending it to that giant balloon.

"Sorry," I mouthed to Charlie when he glanced at me. He puckered his lips as he nodded and wiped the sweat trickling from his neck.

They can. We can.

I grew more and more tired, gasping from the hot air burning into my lungs. My legs ached with their work, but going faster was not an option—it felt like moving through sand. My hands drooped with their heavy duty, but the tug of the mitts held no escape, clinging to me like a second skin. Sam stared at me. His shoulders curled in, and the light painted shadows under his eyes and hollows in his cheeks. My thoughts grew fuzzy as my legs moved back and forth, and my eyes glazed over as I focused on the tubes rising up from my hands in front of me.

Then music floated in the air. A harp. Faint at first, but it grew louder and louder. A melody of a soul crying, and suddenly I couldn't remember why I was here. Or who I was.

The Lost Realm had sucked it out of me.

Chapter Eight

My shift ended, but my legs still felt like they were moving back and forth on the wheel. I hit the floor and stumbled after Sam as he led the way to the bunkhouse. We followed him down dark paths lit by lanterns on poles, sandwiched between guards. Only Charlie's tall figure in front of me gave me the smallest feeling of safety. It had grown darker since I entered the power mill for my shift. The mist now clung to the forest floor leaving the night sky a clear deep plum dotted with stars.

Shadows and fog obscured my way, and I banged into Charlie as we were halted in front of a long, low building. This time I clung to his T-shirt, not wanting to be separated from my one friend here. Guards were posted by the entrance, and around the building's perimeter paced giant, snickering foxes. My eyes were so bleary I couldn't read the words over the door as we were marched into a chilly room. A solitary torch lit the wall, and it spewed smoke, stinging the inside of my nose.

The guards led us through a shower room where we were hosed down with freezing water then dried off in a giant wind tunnel. This rough treatment revived me, and I rocked in place to get warm, but in the huddle of shivering kids I'd lost sight of Charlie until I spotted his head. He was led away with another group. *No!* My insides shook as I was marched away with my own group.

In a large hall we were given bowls of brown glop to eat and ordered to sit at sticky tables on cracked wooden benches. I peered into the soup, expecting to find something nasty like fingernails or mouse turds. I held my breath and slugged down the food. It was greasy and slid down my throat in bitter chunks.

The guard standing at our table glared at me. "Nasty Reekers. Hurry up and eat your gurgle soup. Off you go!"

Back in the bunk room, Sam assigned bed numbers and, after finding my bunk in the near dark, I spread across a bottom bed that smelled like pee. The mattress was just a wool sack stuffed with straw that poked into my back. A worn blanket with ratty holes was crumpled at the bottom of the bed, and I pulled it over my cold legs, squeezing them together for warmth.

I slipped my fingers around the crystal in my pocket and held it tight. In the dark it was hard to make out heads or feet on the other bunks. *Where was Charlie?* Kids whispered around me, some crying. The comfort of my moonlit room back home called to me, where bullfrogs bellowed goodnight and Bo Chez still turned out my light with his dumb baby rhyme. *Nightey nodz and toodley todz, don't let the bedbugs sneak up your snoz.* He'd never mentioned vapes. Or beasts. Bugs I could deal with.

My body craved sleep, but it wouldn't give in yet. Fear kept shaking me awake. Falling asleep on this world might mean never waking up.

"Charlie?" It came out a whisper, desperate for a friendly reply. None came. In all my twelve years I'd never felt so alone, and I tugged the blanket up to my neck.

My eyes adjusted to the darkness. Only one light at the entrance lit this bunkhouse that held hundreds. Guess they didn't want to waste the light on us—the very light we generated. *Hurry up, sleep!* Dreaming was my one form of escape.

"Hey," a voice startled me with a tap on my headboard, and a boy poked his head down. "When'd you get here?"

"Just today, I think."

"I've been here for weeks now." The boy climbed down and plopped on my bed. His chubby body squished next to mine. He looked like a little Bo Chez. A Lo Chez. He even smelled like cheese gone bad.

I sat up. "I've got to get out of here."

"There's a bunch of us planning the same thing."

"I don't belong here."

"Oh, and what, the rest of us do?" He leaned in and poked me in the chest, blowing out a big, stinky cheese breath.

"Sorry, didn't mean that. Are you from here or kidnapped, too?"

"Kidnapped." He sat back and fisted my blanket, frowning at me. "We all were."

The boy whistled long and low. Shapes moved toward us in the dark and kids crowded on my bunk bed.

"This is a new kid," Lo Chez said. "So, newbie, we're figuring out a plan to take Hekate down and escape."

"How?"

"We sneak attack the guards when they do their early morning check, grab their vapes, and kill 'em. Hekate will follow behind them, but we'll vape her, too."

"How will we get home?"

"Her brother, the Child Collector, comes in the morning for his special breakfast the chefs make. We'll kidnap him, threaten to zap him too, and make him send us all home."

The kids nodded at their leader, Lo Chez. Sounded risky to me.

"So are you in or what, new kid?"

"We could die," I said. They just stared at me as if that was obvious. "I've got to get back home to my grandfather."

"We've all got someone to get back home to."

The kid next to Lo Chez started to cry. "My mom's real sick. She's in the hospital and I don't think I'll get to see her again, even if I do get home."

Lo Chez draped his arm on the kid's shoulder. "You'll see her. Right, guys?"

One by one each kid spoke, their dirt and tear-streaked faces floating in the dim light.

"My dad is going overseas in the Army. I wanted to say goodbye."

"My family's going to England to visit my cousins. Don't guess I'm going now."

"We're moving this month. I won't know where to find my family even if I do escape."

The crying kid wiped his nose. "We've all got to get out of here."

I smiled at the kid with fake confidence. "We will."

"Back to your bunks," Lo Chez said. "Wait for the sign."

The kids slunk away, except Lo Chez who darted his eyes around, then focused on me. My fingers slipped to the crystal in my pocket. Share it or not? My heart thudded, trying to decide. I would wait. Besides, could it even help us?

"Are you in?" He thumped my bed.

"Okay." What choice was there? Maybe Charlie was here somewhere too and we could escape together.

"Get some sleep. You'll need it to be ready to go." Lo Chez climbed back on top of his bunk.

He never told me his name, or the others. I don't guess it mattered. We were all the same here, just a brand and a resource for the world of Nostos. And we were lost in this Lost Realm.

I stretched out on my bunk and gave in to the dark. And, finally, in the cramped warmth of my dark prison, sleep dragged me away.

Chapter Nine

Shouts rang out. I jolted up and hit my head on the bunk with a painful whack.

Lo Chez hauled me out. "They're on to us!"

Sleepy-eyed, I stood up. Sam must have turned me in!

"You!" Lo Chez grabbed me, his nose touching mine. "New boy. You told!"

"No, it wasn't me." Terror ran through me. "I swear!"

"Bunk four hundred and two, get over here." Hekate's voice crawled over us.

Lo Chez's frown fell, and he let me go.

Hekate stood outlined in the light from the entrance as Lo Chez made his way to her. *No, don't go!*

The other kids stood in the silent dark.

"You think you can take me down, Reeker?" Hekate said, her voice rising. "I'm older than you know and have more power than you can imagine." Two guards stood beside her. I shrunk into myself, wishing to be anywhere but here.

She grew taller, as if by a magical spell, her shadow rising like a monster on the wall behind her. "Who helped plan your takeover?"

Lo Chez shook his head. "N-no one."

"Liar!" The guards pointed their vapes at his head as the lights flickered, casting ghastly shadows across their faces. The panting of hundreds of kids pulsed around me, and I pressed my fingers into the bunk bed frame, waiting for death to strike.

Hekate held her hands high.

Blue light blazed and the air crackled with electricity and smoke. When it cleared, Lo Chez still stood there.

"Back to your bunks, Reekers." Hekate's shrill voice pierced the air. "No rest for anyone tomorrow unless those involved in this escape plan confess." She turned and left. The guards remained standing at the entrance.

There would be no prison break. The kids skulked back to their beds as I clutched the wobbly bedpost, waiting for Lo Chez to return. He shuffled toward me as his large body moved in and out of the light behind him. Strange moans carried to me. What had she done to him?

Finally, he stood before me, his hands covering his face. Then he clutched my arms. That's when I saw the nightmare that he'd become.

His mouth was gone.

His eyes bulged out with the scream he couldn't voice. It sucked me into a deeper world of horror and held me frozen in its image. His nose flared and he shook all over, shaking me with him. Tears spilled down his cheeks, his mouthless flesh working with silent sobs.

I wrenched away from Lo Chez and fell on my bed, hiding my own face in the scratchy mattress. He crawled on the top bunk, groaning from somewhere deep inside. I felt bad for reacting the way I did, but his monster face freaked me out. There was no comfort here, only work and punishment … death.

Just then, a face popped out from under my bunk. I almost yelled when a hand pulled me by the shirt, yanking me to the floor.

It was Charlie.

And Sam was with him.

Sam put his finger to his mouth. Charlie nodded, then Sam disappeared. I looked to see where he'd gone and felt a cool breeze. A sweaty hand pulled me down into a dark hole under the bed, and Charlie followed close behind.

Our hideaway was dank and damp. My eyes soon adjusted to see a slant of light glowing above. There was a soft creak and a click, and I got a whiff of dead and rotting things as near total darkness covered us.

"What's happening?"

"Shh," Sam whispered back, just an outline before me. "We've got to run. Quick!"

He shot off into the dark with a sack over his shoulders, but I pulled him back by his shirt and handed him my pen flashlight from home, grateful it still worked after my 'shower'—and grateful my mother's photo was laminated and didn't get ruined. Sam hesitated, then took the flashlight from me and moved it around, casting light on the walls as if fascinated, then motioned for us to follow him with his new toy. Charlie shrugged at me from across the shadows, and we ran after our rescuer—if that's what he was.

The dark tunnel seemed to move in and out on either side as we ran. I reached my hands out to the cool walls for balance. Bits of earth brushed off, and who knows what other slimy, squirmy things came with it.

Remembering the crystal, I felt for it in my pocket. It warmed my hand and glowed blue when I pulled it out, like the first time. Charlie bumped into me and gasped when he saw it.

Sam turned around and gasped too. He reached his fingers out toward the crystal, then pulled them away. "A lightning orb!"

I was scared of dropping it now, afraid it would explode like a grenade. Sam's eyes were huge in the blue glow the crystal shed as clouds moved across its tiny space, rolling angry and stormy inside the glass. A spark flared. Charlie backed up and the blue light cast long shadows down his face, which bobbed like a ghost before me.

Sam pointed at my crystal. "How'd you get one?"

I decided to change the subject. "What's in the bag and how'd you get us out?"

Charlie nodded, still staring at the crystal ... or lightning orb.

Sam shook the bag. "Food to keep us going. And I put you and Charlie in the two bunks with secret tunnel doors under them. They've been sealed shut for a long time, but I re-opened them and got your friend for you." He stepped closer then, his eyes widening. "By the gods, I've never seen a lightning orb though, just heard of them. They have great power."

Bo Chez had said so, but how would he have gotten hold of it?

Then Sam added, "Storm Masters from our Sky Realm carry them."

My gut cramped. *Storm Masters were real?* "Sky Realm?"

That's when he said something even stranger. "Zeus rules there. It's where he created the lightning orbs, after he left Mount Olympus."

I bounced from foot to foot, my legs eager to flee while my thoughts paralyzed me. *Mount Olympus was real, too?* But it couldn't be. In school that was mythology, which means "not real."

"*Non! Vraiment?* Mount Olympus like the Greek gods?" Charlie stuck his jaw out as he echoed my thoughts.

Sam nodded, his eyes white moons in the dark. "Vray-what?"

"*Vraiment*. It means 'really'."

"Then, *vraiment*, the Greek gods."

"What can the orb do?" I really didn't want it blowing up in my hand.

"I don't know," Sam said.

Big help.

"Did you steal it?" Sam tilted his head at me.

"From my grandfather."

I wasn't sure how to feel about Bo Chez now, and the fact that this orb—this weapon—had been in our house. This thing from another world—from the Greek gods! They were supposed to have superhuman powers, and this orb of theirs had just been on a shelf over our fireplace.

Sam peered about as if expecting guards to burst upon us any second. "Enough for now. Let's move!"

I pulled him back. "Wait, you need to help me find my other friend, Finn, but I don't know where he is."

"No time for that," Sam said. "I got Charlie here for you as asked."

"Then we don't go with you."

Charlie nodded, following my lead, and crossed him arms. "I'm here because of Joshua and his friend. We can't just leave him."

Sam glanced back and forth between us then sighed. "Fine. We'll find him first. There's only a few places he could be anyways, but time is not on our side."

This all sounded good, but I still didn't know whether to trust him. "Why help us at all?"

"My days are numbered here, and I need a new home."

"New home?"

"I want you to help me escape, too," Sam said.

I glanced at Charlie and then back at Sam. "What do you mean help *you* escape?"

"To a new home with you on Earth."

"But we don't know how to get back."

That's when Sam surprised me even more by saying, "I do."

Chapter Ten

The promise of escape brought me new energy, and we ran in silence for a long time.

Chooga-chooga.

In the feeble light from the flashlight and orb, the tunnel's roof shook over my head as we reached the power mill and ran faster. Chunks of mud fell on my face. I brushed them away, cold and mucky on my fingers.

Long after the sounds of the power mill fled, Sam suddenly stopped. I ran into him, banging my head against his. Charlie ran into me and I dropped the orb, sure we'd all be blasted to bits, but instead, it rolled along the dirt floor like a giant neon marble. Sam snatched it up and curled his fingers tight around it. Had he wanted it all along? Did he really know what it could do? I waited for him to say something as the orb distracted me. He hesitated, then handed it to me.

"Keep it safe. Don't let anyone get ahold of it."

I pushed the orb back in my pocket and wiped the sweat off my face, dying for a fresh breeze to replace the damp tunnel air filling my lungs.

Charlie bent over, hands on his knees, to catch his breath. "Where are we, Sam?"

"Near the end of an old tunnel that once ran between the bakehouse and the power mill. It's not in use anymore and they blocked it off here."

Twittering squeaks punched the air behind us.

"What was that?" I said. Sam swung the flashlight around. It bounced off the walls, and beyond it the black spread deep, ready to suck us up.

"Tunnel rats," Sam said. The squeaks stopped.

"Like the sewer rats?" The Auctioneer's threats came back to me.

He nodded and put a finger to his lips. Charlie and I backed up.

A chitter exploded nearby, and Sam yelled, "Run!"

I needed no motivation, imagining a monster rodent chewing my fingers and nose—and dashed after Sam with Charlie next to me.

The squeaks came faster, angry for having to chase us. I dared a peek behind me. White ghosts danced up and down—only they weren't ghosts at all, but giant rat teeth chomping at us, eager for a bite of boy. Behind those teeth was a determined diner. I was just as determined to not be eaten.

Whiskers scraped the back of my neck and air swished my arms as teeth swiped at us.

"Faster!" I shoved Sam on. Charlie looked behind and yelled, "*Zut! Zut!*"

My tired legs couldn't possibly run faster, but with death at my feet I could fly.

The *chittering* soon faded. My shirt stuck to me with ripe sweat and my lungs burned from our pace, but better to hurt to breathe than not breathe at all.

Sam pointed the flashlight at rungs fastened into the wall and flung himself up them, pushing on a handle above. A door popped open. "Come on!"

Mad clicking of teeth grew closer and I scrambled after him, eager to escape the muddy tunnel. Charlie followed. Sam slammed the lid down. A squeal pierced the air.

Sam cranked the lid handle tight. "It can't get us now," he said.

We found ourselves in woods that stretched out in every direction. The blue sun hung over us in an early morning lavender sky as tentacles of fog reached up to grab it. The mist rolled heavy on the forest floor, slinking between crooked trees that offered up their broken arms to the sky and to the earth where they curved down like protective robes. These gray and white cobbled trees stood like old wizards who'd lost their magical power and were left here to die. Goosebumps shot down my arms from the creepy woods, but it was better than the power mill.

I flung myself on the ground, leaned against a tree to catch my breath, and ran my fingers over the furry moss that smelled of fresh-cut grass. A piece of home.

Charlie flopped down beside me, breathing heavy. "*Très fatigué!* Must rest."

Sam hesitated, looking around. "Not for long."

"Starving!" Charlie groaned, holding his belly.

"Yeah," I said. "What's in that bag?"

Sam drew out what looked like corn dogs and the biscuits I'd eaten in the power mill. "Slug dogs and bong bongs."

Charlie and I grabbed a slug dog each and chowed down. Sweet and crunchy.

"What are they?" I licked my fingers.

"Boiled slugs, dipped in honey, rolled in crushed acorns, and fried."

I swallowed hard and Charlie and I cringed at each other. "And the bong bongs?"

"Made from the bong bong tree berry. The shell is crushed to make flour and formed in a ball then the berries are stuffed inside."

That sounded better. They hadn't tasted bad in the power mill, just dry. I shoved one down now and chugged water from Sam's canteen then passed it to Charlie. After my stomach was full I pulled out my pencil and rolled it between my fingers. Drawing always helped me forget things back home when I was upset, and so I drew here on the birch bark of this giant tree. My fingers knew what to draw. It was what Finn and I had talked about making many times: our fort. We dreamed of building it just like a real castle with towers to hide in, flags, and a moat to protect us. I signed it *Joshua was here.*

"Pretty good," Charlie said, leaning in. "I wish my dad let me take art lessons." He pulled at a thread on his ripped shirt. "There was a comic book camp at school but I had to do basketball instead."

"Here. Try." I handed him the pencil. "Add to mine."

He studied the pencil, then drew trees around the castle and two figures, one short and one tall, running after his friend. And under *Joshua was here* he added *Charlie too*.

He thrust the pencil back at me and tilted his head, bangs covering one eye. "Pretty pathetic."

"You just need practice, and now someone will know we were both here together," I said, and his face brightened at that.

"Looks like King Apollo's castle," Sam said, glancing at it, and then in an instant pulled us both up. "Let's go."

We trotted after him, but Charlie twisted his ankle and I caught him before he cracked his head into a tree. He cried out and put his full weight on my arm, favoring his good foot, as he hobbled forward.

"I'll be okay," he said with a pinched face.

"You need better shoes," I said.

"Yeah, well that will never happen."

"How come?"

"We don't have the money. All my parents do is fight about it."

"Oh," I said, sorry I mentioned it.

"I always wanted American brand names like the rich kids at my school. Like you." He pointed at my clothes and shoes. "But my parents are poor. We live in a tiny apartment so I can go to a good school. I hate it." He crumpled his hands in fists.

My clothes were something I didn't think much about. Bo Chez bought me what I wanted as long as it was on sale.

Sam hurried back to us now, and Charlie put more weight on his foot.

"All right?"

Charlie nodded and we took off, a bit slower this time.

I took the slowed pace to dig at Sam for more information. "Are there really Greek gods here?"

He shook his head, switching the food bag to another shoulder. "Not anymore. They fell from power long ago, abandoned Mount Olympus, and lost their immortality." He blew out a big breath, pushing the never ending mist away. "And now the descendants of the gods rule our lands, like Apollo's heir runs the Lost Realm and—" Sam sniffed the air and looked wildly about. "Come on!"

He pulled us into the woods and we stumbled after him, the words *Mount Olympus* and *Apollo's heir* still bursting in my head. This time I set the pace, mindful of Charlie's sore ankle, peering behind me every few seconds to scan the woods for monsters at our back. My eyes darted to the treetops, expecting a freaky beast to jump on my back and tear me apart.

"How far until we find Finn?"

"We're in Cypress Woods now," Sam said in

between breaths as we ran. "Your friend is at one of the workhouses or the castle. The bakehouse is closest. Either way, we have to go over Mount Parnassus to find him. It's two hours by horse on the road so will be longer on foot."

A mournful coo called in the distance. Another one responded. The mist licked around me like a gray flame and sharp pains pulled at my sides.

"Your friend isn't the only reason to hurry," Sam said. "We've got to get deep into the woods and take cover. Spies are all around."

His voice lowered and took on a more ominous tone. "If they find out we're missing before breakfast, we might not make it."

***

We lifted unwilling legs up over the tree stumps and straggled over streams where strange things moved about. A fin pushed up from one. A tail flipped from another. Water splashed my jeans, cold and stinging. After that I leapt higher over them, fearful of being pulled down by a watery monster.

The quiet was unsettling with just the thuds of our feet on the mossy ground and the dead trees creaking in the breeze as they towered above. They seemed to move their arms in the mist, reaching out for us as if we could bring them to life. We ran through their graveyard, climbing higher and higher. The floor of the woods spread out as we moved up the mountain. There was no path, but Sam ran as if he knew exactly where he was headed. Finally, he stopped.

"Where are we?" A stitch tugged at my side with a worsening throb, and I was terribly thirsty.

"The Spring of Galene." He pointed to a pile of rocks. Water bubbled from the top of the big rock in the middle and flowed down into a shiny basin. "A fabled spring that rejuvenates strangers on a long journey."

Charlie nodded. "But is it safe to drink? Nothing *mysterieux* swimming about in it?" He must've noticed the stream-creatures, too.

Sam nodded and picked up a round leaf. He cupped it under the bubbling water and filled it up. He handed it to me, but I hesitated even though my tongue was stuck to the roof of my mouth like a piece of paper. Sam shrugged and drank greedily, then Charlie drank. I finally took the leaf and drank too. A hint of sweet honey lingered on my tongue and flowed through me with healing warmth as energy surged in me.

"What was the real god Apollo like?" I said as Sam filled up the canteen from the spring.

Sam smiled, and it looked strange on his sad face. "He was the god of light, truth, music, and healing. They said he could prophesize the future, and he taught your people about medicine." His face fell then. "But he was also the god of plagues and death like his twin Artemis."

What was Sam's role here that he knew so much? "How do you about all this?"

"*Oui*," Charlie said with a frown.

Sam didn't answer, then opened his mouth as if to tell us but stiffened, sniffed the air, and waved a hand our way. "Let's go! The cadmean beasts are close."

We could only go so fast. The mist spread thick through the ash colored woods, and somewhere beyond the nothingness could be giant, red-eyed beasts eager to rip us apart.

It wasn't long until Sam stopped fast and took a deep sniff. "By the gods, hurry!"

He turned to his left and ran. Charlie and I were right behind him when a snarl cut through the silent vapor.

A pair of red eyes burned down at us. Then another. And another.

Trouble was here—stalking us through the mist.

Chapter Eleven

Charlie, Sam, and I backed up to one another. Three cadmean beasts glared down at us, their mouths dripping with red foam. I didn't want to be part of that foam.

The tallest one pricked its ears back and forth, and then snorted. Its breath pulsed in the air to the beat of its paw thumping the ground as curved claws scraped deep lines in the dirt.

"Don't hurt us," I said out loud. Instinct drove me to keep talking. "Leave us alone and we'll leave you alone."

The leader threw its nose up in the air and howled.

"You're just making it mad," Charlie said as he and Sam backed away.

The beast spoke, and to my shock, I understood him clearly. "As if you runts could do anything to us. We rule this forest, Reeker meat."

The other beasts joined their leader in mocking us.

"Reeker meat! Reeker meat!"

"Joshua—" Sam whispered behind me, but I cut him off with a glance.

"We're not Reeker meat."

"What?" Sam and Charlie's mouths hung open. The beasts stepped forward. We all stepped back.

"*Mon dieu*," Charlie said. "Why did you say that?"

"Didn't you hear them?" I said.

Sam and Charlie's gaze flicked to the beasts and back to me again.

"You're a malumpus-tongue," Sam said, as if that had some meaning to me.

I was as shocked as they. If beasts could smile and talk on this world, what else could they do? The beasts continued to laugh.

Charlie said, "What the h—"

"And they're *not* friendly," I whispered.

Charlie backed up further as he held onto my shirt, pulling it tight against my skin. "I didn't think they wanted to play catch." A branch snapped underfoot and we both flinched.

The trees crowded around us, the deafening quiet of the woods pounding in my ears. Sweat broke out on my lip and I wiped it away. The one beast licked its lips in return, then curled its mouth in an awful grin, exposing vampire dagger teeth.

The beasts inched toward us. "We don't want to hurt you." Bluffing still seemed the best idea.

"And you won't, my tasty morsels." The leader panted hungrily.

The lightning orb. I had to trust in Bo Chez's story and believe all its stormy, electric power could help us. But Sam had said the Greek gods lost their powers. *Let it do something! And if it breaks, I'm sorry, Bo Chez!*

Charlie clung to my arm so tight it cramped. Fire flashed out of the leader's mouth, and a long flame roared toward us, cutting through the mist like a fire sword. All three of us stumbled back.

The beast pack leapt toward us like hairy dragons. The moss beneath our feet snapped with fire and heat roasted my face and arms. Fire raced up the wizard trees, and their wood shrieked in splitting agony.

"Run!" Sam dragged Charlie and me back.

Red eyes glared at me.

"Hi-yahh!" I flung the orb hard.

Blue light exploded into the space before us and knocked us all off our feet. I slammed sideways into a tree and slid down to the ground. The beasts were sprawled motionless before us on the blackened, smoldering moss. Trees smoked as flames flickered up them. Charlie and Sam lay a few feet away. We all staggered up.

My arm was numb from the shock of hitting the tree and my legs ached. The air sizzled. The sickening smell of burnt fur snaked up my nose, and my legs grew less wobbly as the fear that had gripped me drained away.

Something sailed toward me through the air. It twisted and rolled along in slow motion.

The orb.

"Joshua, it's coming back to you," Sam said. The orb hovered before me and fell into my hand, cool and comforting. Its blue glow dimmed as I gripped it so hard my nails cut into my palm. Sparks flared across my fingertips. Charlie moved closer to me. Blood trickled down his forehead.

"I guess the legend is true. It always goes back to the hand that throws it," Sam said.

"If you had instructions, we sure could have used them earlier," I said.

"Sorry. How did you know to throw it?"

"It just felt ... right."

"You know a lot of stuff," Charlie said, his eyes wide. I squirmed, not liking the way he and Sam were staring at me.

Sam tipped his head. "Well, we know now what you can do, Joshua, and that's what counts." He squinted at me. "You're from Earth?"

"Where the heck else would I be from?" I rubbed my temple back and forth, feeling light-headed from the smoke and all that had just happened.

"I'll tell you this," Sam said. "Of all the people in our twelve realms, only those with the ancient power from the Arrow Realm have the malumpus-tongue."

"What's that mean?" Not sure if I wanted to know.

"Talk to animals."

"You mean you didn't hear them talk?"

Sam shook his head and Charlie crossed his arms, raising an eyebrow. "And I thought only Doctor Doolittle talked to the animals."

"You hear animals speak on Earth?" Sam said, his black eyes huge in his pale face.

"No. How could I?"

"Maybe the orb gives you powers here."

I stared at the orb, wondering how I was connected to this place. For the first time, an idea forced its way into my head that maybe I wasn't here by chance. *Bo Chez, find me!* But how could he?

Movement caught my eye. Two of the beasts stirred. "They're not all dead," Sam said.

I pushed the orb deep into my pocket and muttered, "Let's go."

The fire from the cadmean beasts' mouths was my inspiration as my leaden legs pushed forward. We soon reached a fast running creek, the smell of singed wood and hair behind us.

Sam gestured to the rushing water. "We can't cross here."

"Well, I am," I said as I waded through water that reached my knees. There were no fire-breathing foxes here, and that was good enough for me. Beyond the tumbling froth spread a heavy gray curtain of fog. Charlie and Sam both hesitated.

"What are you waiting for?" I shouted, urgency pushing me on like the water swirling around my waist. Charlie flitted his eyes up and down the creek, then ran in behind me.

"The creeks aren't safe," Sam yelled back.

"Nothing is here." I'd almost reached the other side with Charlie on top of me.

"For the love of Olympus," Sam said and charged in the water. "All right!"

Charlie and I neared the bank, his hand on my back nudging me along through the frigid water. Sensing someone watching me, I searched over my shoulder for red eyes, but there were none. We scrambled up the bank just as a snout poked its head up out of the water behind me.

Sam pointed. "We can head this way a bit and up to the top of Mount Parnassus. Down the other side is the bakehouse. I've only taken the road to get there, but we're heading in the right direction."

"Sounds easy enough," I said, stamping my soggy feet to warm them up.

"As long as we don't come across any Perimeter People," Sam said.

"Who are they?" Charlie looked around as if such people were after us now.

"Outcasts, mostly. People who've been banished across Nostos for not following laws. Some people choose to come here and live a life without laws. Sometimes a ruler will send in guards and cadmean beasts to sweep the Perimeter Lands and toss a few off The Edge."

Charlie scowled. "The edge of what?"

"Of our world," Sam said matter-of-factly. "It's flat. You drop off and never come back."

I snorted. "Isn't Apollo ruler of the sun? So why doesn't he just drag them off The Edge with his chariot?"

Sam turned to me. "I told you. The gods lost their power. And he's not the original Apollo. He died long ago. Each new king takes on the Apollo name."

"Whatever. I just want to get my friend," I said and took off running, spurred on by Finn's face in my head. Charlie and Sam scrambled to keep up.

I dragged my legs over logs and rocks, my wet pants clinging to me like weights, wondering where Finn might be and what he was being forced to do. Was he trying to escape, too, in this land of the fallen Greek gods?

With the cadmean beasts long behind, Sam slowed down a bit, sniffed the air, and gave me a weary smile as if confirming we had lost our pursuers. The trees grew together, protecting me, hiding me from what chased us, and my anxiety lessened. At one point the woods were so dense we had to walk single file. I brought up the rear with a feeling of safety covering me as thick as the mist.

It was then that a rough hand closed on my throat, and cold steel pushed into my neck.

Chapter Twelve

I stood like a statue, the knife at my throat pricking my skin with a thorny sting. The man smelled like wet leaves mixed with leather and chocolate. It wasn't unpleasant, but the fact he could kill me with a flick of his hand was. Sam and Charlie both turned around and froze as well. My heart raced so fast I thought it would leap out of my mouth and flop onto the forest floor.

The man grabbed my arm with his other hand, twisting my brand. "You're Lost Realm Reekers."

None of us answered.

"You." The man pointed at Charlie. "Tell me what you boys are doing in the Perimeter Lands." His voice sliced the silence.

Charlie cleared his throat. "Trying to get to the bakehouse."

A tickle threatened to turn into a sneeze, but the knife eased off my neck a bit.

"That's all, eh? And how is it you came to be here, my young friends?" the man said, his body like an oven up against mine.

Charlie and Sam glanced sideways at each other.

I took a chance, speaking through tight lips so my throat didn't get cut. "We escaped from the power mill, and we're on our way to rescue my friend Finn and get back to Earth."

Sam gave me a look that told me to shut up.

But the man pulled the knife off my neck and shoved me away from him, toward Sam and Charlie. I stumbled and turned around to face him. He was tall and thin, and stood fierce before us, feet planted hip-width apart, as he tapped his fisted knuckles at his waist. Arrows poked out of a quiver hanging from his back, and a bow was slung across his chest. His hooded cloak gleamed with mist and fell to the tops of his cracked leather boots. He pushed his cloak aside just enough to tuck the knife into a sheathe that was strapped on one leg with a fancy letter "L" scrolled across the top of it. His long brown hair was streaked with white and twisted into ropes that swayed across half of his face. And when he brushed it away impatiently, it revealed a long scar that ran from his hairline to his chin. Was he a fallen god, too? He looked like one with his sharp nose and angled face.

He frowned at me. "And how do you propose you'll get back to Earth if you succeed in this rescue folly?"

Charlie and I looked at Sam, who hadn't come clean about that part yet. Sam just shook his head, and the man returned his hand to his knife. I slowly slid my hand in my pocket and gripped the orb so hard my fingers tingled.

Sam sighed. "With a Lightning Gate key."

I didn't know what a Lightning Gate key was, but Sam acted as if revealing this bit of information was like pulling out one of his teeth. Maybe he didn't trust this guy, but there was something in the man that drew me to him. I felt—somehow—he wouldn't harm us.

The man waved a hand at Sam. "And how would you know where to get such a key?"

Sam blew out an even longer sigh. "My mother was one of King Apollo's wives."

Charlie grabbed my arm as I worked to scrape my jaw off the ground. Sam was a prince of a fallen Greek god? And he wanted *us* to help *him*? And why would a prince want to escape from his kingdom?

"So?" the man said.

Sam kicked at the dirt, looking miserable. "Living in the castle has its advantages when it comes to discovering things."

"You have this Lightning Gate key?" the man said, stepping toward us and thrusting his hand open. "In that bag perhaps?" In just a few questions, he'd pried more from Sam than we'd learned in a day. And the more he revealed, the more our escape took shape. I nodded to Sam, eager to hear that we would soon be on our way home.

Sam shook his head. "Just slug dogs and bong bongs in here."

The man grabbed the bag to make sure then threw it back.

"And the only person who has a key is a Child Collector," Sam said.

My hopes sank. I had no interest in ever crossing paths with that nasty dude again. There must be another way.

"I know." The man flipped his cloak behind him, revealing a brown belt that wrapped around his slim waist encrusted with colored squares covered in letters and numbers.

It seemed familiar, and then Sam shook a finger at the man. "That's a Child Collector's belt!" He backed up, and Charlie and I went with him, fear of being taken again crashing through me.

But the man just smiled at us. "Have no fear, boys."

"You're a Taker, then?" Sam took another step back. That didn't sound good either.

"Afraid not."

"What are you going to do to us?" The suspense was killing me, and I bent my knees, feet ready to run.

"I may have some other use for you besides turning you in to Hekate."

He made no move to capture us so I dared a question. "What does the belt do?"

Sam answered for the man. "It allows a Child Collector to travel to Earth, choose a destination, and return to Nostos." He yanked his baggy shirt down, balling it up in his hands. "Only after he's scoured his assigned Earth region looking for kids to steal that is."

"This is true," the man said, cocking his head with pursed lips, having fun with us. "The Lightning Gate can pinpoint an Earth region, but my belt allows me to choose a specific destination."

"Like where?" I said.

"A country or town—or even an address—on Earth or Nostos."

Sam flicked a finger at the man. "And once a Collector visits there and sources out new slaves he catalogues their locations and returns to take them one by one."

"Nice recitation from your schooling, boy."

"And each realm is assigned specific Earth countries. Our realm is France, England, and America," Sam continued, spitting out each word. "So where are you assigned, Collector?"

The man let his fingers slide over the belt buttons. "That is none of your concern," he said evenly, and then he pointed at Sam. "Enough of today's lesson! Back to business. Do you at least have the codes to go with the key?"

"Not exactly," Sam said, slumping his shoulders.

"Describe 'not exactly.'"

"The king keeps the codes in the Castle. *You* would know that. And you should have your own key and codes, *Child Collector*." He flung his fingers at the man.

"Maybe I do. And maybe I don't." The man's jaw twitched, and he took a step closer, placing a hand on his knife. "But I want to know how *you* planned to go about getting them. Your answer may mean the difference between staying free, or not."

"Once we find his friend"—Sam jerked a thumb at me—"we planned to steal the codes from the castle, and then steal a gate key from the Child Collector's supply in his house. I know where he lives. I'd steal his code set too, but he keeps it on him, and I'm not keen to search his pockets. Or yours."

The man dropped his menacing look and laughed. "I give you marks for bravery, daring to step into a Child Collector's abode, but how did you plan to get the codes from King Apollo? You thought the king would just hand them over if you asked politely?"

"Why bother with all this?" Sam said with a groan. "If you're not going to turn us over to Hekate then just let us go on our way."

But I had another mission for the man. "Will you help us get to Earth?"

Chapter Thirteen

Charlie and Sam gaped at me as if my head had twisted around backward. The guy was a Child Collector and just held a knife to my throat—even I couldn't justify why I'd asked—but we had few options and taking risks seemed to be working here.

The man folded his arms and thought for a moment. "Perhaps." Our captor smirked at Sam. "So, Prince, convince me why I should help you or let you go. There's a reward in it for me, after all, if I bring you back to my realm."

Sam remained tight-lipped. The man stepped forward and put a hand again to the handle of his knife.

Sam turned red and sighed with defeat. "My mother lost favor with King Apollo and was banished from the Lost Realm to Earth. I was raised there and want to go back and find her, or at least a new home with one of these two."

"Your mom lives on Earth?" I said. Sam's story got stranger and stranger. "How—"

"Wait." The man put out his hand to cut me off. "Prince, does this code set you plan to steal have all the travel codes, including the Earth one? Or just merchant transport codes to travel between realms?"

Sam scrunched his face up. "Why do you need to know that? You must have your own set! Or did you lose them and your gate key and you're afraid of getting punished for it?"

I feared Sam had gone too far this time, but the man tilted his head and laughed. A deep, booming laugh that echoed around us. "You boys have heart, I grant you. But this is a time of great unrest, and Lost Realm folk fear the Dark Ages returning. Plus, you should be kinder to me if you want my help. And you have much to learn about traversing the Perimeter Lands. You make one move in the wrong direction and off you go. Over The Edge. Into The Great Beyond. Do you know what happens next?"

At the same time Sam nodded, I shook my head.

"You fall through space until you die of hunger and thirst. Then you float around forever. If you're lucky, you shoot through a wormhole and crash down onto another Nostos realm before you die. If not, all that's left will be your bones rattling together in space."

It all sounded like some wild story to me, even on this place. Yet the purple sky, blue sun, and the mist that held flame-throwing beasts made anything a possibility.

"How do you know about wormholes?" Sam said.

"By the arrow of Artemis, I've seen one!" The man hurled a fist in Sam's face. "And it's not just The Edge you have to worry about."

Sam shrugged. "We've dealt with the cadmean beasts. We can deal with the rest."

The man's expression tightened. "Perhaps. But what about the hydriads? They roam the Acheron creeks seeking prey to suck the water from their body."

A memory of Sam's fear of the creek, a snout rising above the water, and that feeling of being watched popped in my head, and my skin prickled. Danger lurked everywhere in this place. If I ever got home again I would cherish every minute being bored. Bored was better than dead.

"So, we'll find a way around and won't cross anymore creeks," I said with more confidence than I felt.

"You have no choice. The Acheron creeks crisscross the entire Perimeter Lands."

A biting breeze rushed over me, and its roar blew by like the very creek we'd crossed. We needed a friend, and this man might be a Child Collector, but he was listening to us and hadn't blasted us yet—and he may have a way home. I raised my hand. "Listen, whatever your name is—"

"Call me Leandro."

"Leandro. Why share this?" The man's eyes were like a dark green sea mixed with blue, one eye shining bluer than the other.

"Because I can help you find your friend. And maybe get back to Earth."

"And why help us?" I needed to trust him completely.

The man looked at me for a long while. His eyes shone intensely and held a yearning and power that scared me. He flung his hair back, and the scar on his face zig-zagged white across his skin. Finally, he answered. "Because I travel between realms searching for someone as well. Two someones. I want to get to Earth, too, but first must find my people. In helping you, perhaps I'll find mine … and find a way to Earth."

"You *don't* have the codes to get to Earth then," Sam said. The man said nothing, just crossed his arms.

"You've fallen away," Sam said, more like a question this time. Still silence.

Sam, Charlie, and I nodded in agreement. This man was our one choice.

Leandro took our nods as approval and broke the silence. "I come from the Arrow Realm, ruled by the once-great hunter goddess, Artemis. And if you don't quarrel with me, we won't have a problem."

With that, we all relaxed a bit and introduced ourselves. Leandro's gaze held mine as he shook my hand. His palm had ridges on it like it had fought often and worked hard. I was the one who finally looked away. There was nothing fallen about him. He seemed god-like to me.

A horn trumpeted through the quiet woods. Three times. Its echo rang around us.

"The alert," Sam said. "They'll be looking for us now."

"Even if they did catch us, with you being a prince and all, maybe they'll go easy on us," I said. It sounded good to me.

Sam shook his head. "I'm a traitor now, an ignorant Barbaros like you. I helped Reekers escape. Anyway, I have no special privileges. King Apollo does not favor me." He said no more on the subject.

"That's not all who'll be looking for us. The cadmean beasts know we're in here too," Charlie reminded us. I glanced around us, expecting some new and unimagined horror to lunge at us, or a vine to grab my leg and drag me down into the dark earth and bury me forever. Anything could happen here. What would be next?

"Then we must head over the mountain now and find your friend," Leandro said. "The bakehouse is half a day's journey on foot from here."

We were off once more, but Sam held me back as we slow-jogged, and he whispered in my ear. "He could be leading us right to Hekate or the king. And if we're caught, we're dead."

"I don't think so. He could have killed us already," I whispered back.

"*Oui*," Charlie jumped in. "I'm with Joshua."

"We can take him down," Sam said. "Three against one."

"We wouldn't win," I argued in-between breaths.

"Then let's run," Sam said. "He can only catch one

of us. Two of us would escape."

I shook my head. "We need him."

"We can do this on our own," Sam said, his voice rising.

"I trust him."

Charlie nodded, eager to follow along with me.

Leandro flashed us a stern look to catch up, and we all moved faster. My pant legs were almost dry, and I warmed up as we ran after Leandro, trying to match his pace as he dashed around trees. His heavy boots crushed fallen branches, and his cloak flowed behind him like a magic carpet. The air he stirred rushed past me with his earthy chocolate smell. Even though he had held a knife against my throat, I held no grudge against him. Not in this place. He had reason to be cautious.

He was a good man. A man I wanted to follow.

Chapter Fourteen

"There." Leandro pointed ahead of us. "Where the light spreads out is The Edge. We go no further that way."

We'd been walking for what seemed like hours. Leandro had allowed brief stops to eat and drink but not long enough for me. We finished Sam's slug dogs and bong bongs, and at each break I quickly left my mark on this world with pictures of home. Part of me wanted to believe Bo Chez would come for me. If he did, would he find me through the trees that now told the story of the people and places in my life?

Another stop would be good as cramps shot through my calves, but Leandro had no idea to rest this time. "We must continue heading north, up and over Mount Parnassus. It's perilous enough traveling the roads between realms filled with banished folk and thieves, much less these Perimeter Lands. Let's hope we don't run into strangers here with unwelcome agendas."

He spoke too soon.

Three such strangers dropped from the trees, their swords pointed at us. Each had grimy long hair, stained cloaks, and wore Child Collector belts.

Leandro's nostrils flared and he pulled out his knife, ready for a fight. Charlie, Sam, and I crept backward together.

"Stop right there, boys," the one man said, his lips in a tight line.

Leandro puffed his chest out and brandished his knife. "We have no dispute with you. We merely want to cross over the mountain."

"What's in it for us if we let you?" The leader stole a look at his friends.

"I let you live, that's what in it for you." Leandro put his knife away. The men relaxed and dropped their swords. In a blur, Leandro's cloak flashed open and he pulled off his bow and set an arrow to it, aiming it at the leader's chest. Our attackers' smiles faded, and they each took a wider stance. The leader raised his sword again. It sliced through the fog that curled along the glinting steel.

"I saw your belt, Child Collector." The leader moved toward Leandro, slashing his sword at him. "Do you know who we are?"

"Takers."

"Good guess, child thief. And we're here to stop your kind."

"Don't force me to hurt you," Leandro said in a calm voice. "I'm trained to fight the likes of you."

The man bared his teeth and flexed his arms. "And now you're here with your nasty new recruits." His eyes shrunk into black slits. "We heard the alarm. You're on a training hunt, is that it?"

"We're here hunting too," the skinny one said, leering at Leandro. "No more lightning roads for you."

Leandro drew back his bow, his arm steady. The men stepped in closer, and their unwashed stink mixed with my own rising sweat and fog that clung to my skin. I grasped the orb in my pocket, my pulse throbbing into it.

"You monsters stole a boy from each of us," the leader said. "But we've taken from you, too, killed your own. And now we're here to find our sons."

Confusion spilled through me. *Weren't they Child Collectors, too?*

"We're not Child Collectors," I blurted out. "Tell them, Leandro! We're kids from Earth."

"Shut up." The leader waved his sword at me. "You would be at one of the workhouses if you were."

Leandro didn't respond, his arrow ready to fly. The veins in his hands popped as he pulled the bow's string tighter.

The other men stepped forward, raising their swords high, and the trees crowded us in, no longer offering safety as they pushed us closer toward our new enemy.

"Before we kill you, we want all your weapons,

including your travel belt, and that lovely cloak." The leader punched his sword at Leandro.

We had one hope: the orb. But could we fully trust Leandro? Once he knew of it, would he steal it and slit my throat as first promised? But we must have some purpose for him—and he hadn't killed us yet.

But then Leandro lowered his bow and smiled at the men. "Seems you outnumber my weapons here. I was hoping to trade these boys in for a reward, but you can have them. They're more trouble than they're worth."

He shoved Sam, Charlie, and I toward the bandits.

Then, quick as lightning, each of the three men grabbed one of us.

The leader gripped me tight, ragged nails cutting into my skin. "Figures you betray your own kind, monster."

The other two held Sam and Charlie to their sides. I struggled to get away and grab the orb again, but the grip of my captor was too strong. Leandro slung his bow across his chest and put his hands on his waist. Sam was right. How wrong we were to trust him.

"Joshua, do something!" Charlie struggled with no effect, and his captor roared with laughter at his efforts. There was no way to get the orb with my closest arm painfully pressed into my side.

Leandro tossed his head back and laughed. "Go ahead. Throw them over. That's the fun part."

"Fun until it's your turn," my captor said, stepping back with the others.

But Leandro just smiled as anger and fear at his traitorous act boiled inside me. "Oh, I don't think so." The men cast puzzled glances to one another but continued to lug us to The Edge. I tried to dig my feet into the ground, scraping rocks along as I struggled, but the man's grip was unbreakable. The purple sky of The Great Beyond waited to float me away forever with the bones of the dead or shoot me through a wormhole.

Leandro kept pace with them. Step by step he moved to The Edge with us. I now gripped the hand that clutched me, as it held me out closer into The Great Beyond. Charlie screamed, but Sam remained silent. He peered at me from above his captor's fist.

"We're trying to get back to Earth," I pleaded. "Look at my brand, you idiots!" My foot slipped off The Edge and I yanked it in, clinging to my captor.

"Lies! Anyone could make that mark. Now shut your mouth," the leader said, jiggling me for emphasis.

"Well, go on then," Leandro prodded them with a sneer. *Oh, why didn't he just leave?*

All three bandits leaned us further over The Edge. I dared a peek behind me. A skull floated past. A skeleton hand swirled as if waving. Vast purple space waited to claim me, its stars peeking through the endless void. The blue sun slipped below the edge and the orange moon rose low on the horizon, delivering another night.

Chapter Fifteen

We were going to die. Before finding Finn. Before seeing Bo Chez again. All this for nothing.

And then anger overrode my fear.

I bit my enemy's hand. Charlie and Sam took my lead and did the same thing. All three men yelled in surprise and threw us down. We fell on sweet dirt and dragged ourselves forward.

As Leandro pulled all three of us in by our collars, I tugged out the orb and threw it at the men who sprung at us. They dodged. *Dang! Missed!* A blue-white explosion blazed, and a whiff of hot metal seared my nose. I hugged the ground and the startled men toppled over The Edge, reaching out for us.

The bandits fell.

And so did Charlie, Sam, and I—snatched by these Takers.

Leandro's face hovered above, and I reached out

my arms to grab him. But there was nothing. Screams filled the air. *Were they mine?* I kicked at the hand that held me. It let go. I floated slowly down into space, as if a force field surrounded me. The crisp scent of a hot pavement after rain struck me, and I heaved in great breaths, fearful the air would run out.

Leandro swung his arm out in a wide arc. A hot rope wound around my waist, seizing me to a stop, along with Sam and Charlie who clung tight to me. Charlie was crying and Sam's head was bent over my shoulder. We rose through the air, pressed to each other, our body heat pumping thick between us. The muscles in Leandro's neck bulged as he hauled us up until we stood next to him on the ground again and he unwound the long whip that bound us.

"You saved us." I fell, hard, on the ground, my legs too shaky to stand.

"They screamed all the way down." Sam peered over The Edge.

"I hope they're still screaming like a bunch of babies." Charlie wiped his face. It was over. We were alive.

Leandro looked at us with kind eyes. "All right, boys?"

We nodded. Leandro coiled his whip up and clipped it to the back of his belt under his cloak. "A fire belt. Grows as long as you need it and works better than any lasso."

He never intended for us to die, but my insides still quivered. I'd lost my friend, been stolen from my home, made to work as a slave, on the run for my life, and was nearly killed by beasts and thieves. I'd experienced enough adventure for a lifetime in this place.

"Joshua, look." Sam pointed behind me.

The orb came into view just beyond The Edge. It moved through the air in a direct path back to me. It fell onto my palm, its blue glow comforting me.

Leandro put his warm hand over mine, so many questions in his eyes. Was he going to steal the orb? I looked up at him, eager for him to be what I wanted him to be.

"Better put that away for now, Joshua. You can tell me another time how it came to be in your possession."

I did as he said and slid it deep into my pocket.

"It's best we keep moving," Leandro said. "There could be others." Sam, Charlie, and I just stood there, too shook up to move. Three horns blew again. Staying here was not an option.

Leandro studied us for a moment. "I think it's time to try for some different transport, don't you, boys?"

Leandro called to the sky, "We need your help, great golden ones." Through the treetops, shadowy figures headed toward us. They moved silently, floating down. Four brown stags riding the air. They flattened their hooves and landed before us with antlers of sparkling gold.

Leandro bent his head toward the deer.

"Kernitians," Sam said knowingly. "They're wild and unpredictable, but can help folks in need." He smiled at Leandro for the first time. The man could conjure animals from thin air. Impressive.

Leandro pulled us toward the deer. "Quickly."

"We're supposed to ride these … ker-nee-chins?" Charlie squinted at the giant antlers that spun like glittery fingers from the creature's heads.

"Would you rather walk with what's on land?" Leandro looked at Charlie, hands on his hips. He wasn't a big man, but his mass seemed to fill the space between the trees. We all shook our heads. "We'll have to fly high so we aren't seen."

A kernitian grunted "hello" at me. *These kernitians could talk to me too?*

It bent its head. I placed my hand on its smooth neck and swung up onto its back. It wasn't as tall as a horse, but large muscles rippled down its back and flanks. I hugged its neck, breathing in its lemon-pepper smell. "Thank you."

"You're welcome," it said, and I understood it perfectly.

Leandro watched me with narrowed eyes, but there was no explanation to give him. Charlie, Sam, and Leandro mounted their kernitians as well.

Then Leandro leaned in and said something to his ride that whinnied back to him. "He agrees with me."

I shrugged. "About what?"

"That you could be one of us, malumpus-boy," Leandro said.

Anger and exhaustion rolled through me, wanting to just go to sleep and wake up at home. "I'm just a

Reeker, remember? An ignorant Barbaros! And one you were about to have tossed off The Edge!"

I glared at Leandro, but he just laughed. "Better than being a Taker at the moment."

And with that we lifted off the ground. A steady breeze pumped over us, and I drew warmth from my ride as shapes moved below us in the woods. Cadmean beasts or more Takers to attack us? It didn't matter now as the safety of the sky surrounded us. The setting blue sun glowed sadly in the purple distance, then fell away. Up here it was clear of mist, and stars twinkled and grew bright as the orange moon peeked higher.

"Who are these Takers, and how'd they get here?" I asked Leandro.

"Misguided Earth folks who lurk in the Perimeter Lands and have discovered what we do. They've banded together to lure Child Collectors on Earth, kill them, and use their travel belts to come here and find their missing children—and continue killing."

"They're known across the Perimeter Lands of Nostos," Sam said. "Each realm can be two- to three-days' ride by horse from each other, and in between are miles and miles of empty woods, jungle, tundra, or desert, so plenty of room to hide. Zeus orders each realm to empty out the Perimeter Lands once a year and toss vagrants off The Edge."

"But he can't catch them all," Charlie said, with hope, and Sam shook his head.

We had heroes on our side. "So they're good guys too?"

"For your purposes, mostly," Leandro said. "But some have crossed over into crazed lawlessness and are dangerous to all, mortal or not. As you can see, they did not believe you were mortals and would have slit your throats as readily as mine."

Nothing was as it seemed here, not even people from my own world. "Is that what you are then?" He didn't answer, but I kept at him. "You're not a Child Collector either are you, Leandro?"

He kept quiet, guarding his secret.

We rose up to the treetops and beyond. Far away, mountains poked up from the trees as we flew over scattered cottages. No people appeared, only a few wisps of smoke curling from chimneys in this medieval world that held castles, kings, and slaves.

Up ahead, Leandro led the way. His cloak flew around him like a great warrior riding his horse into an unknown battle.

But could he help us win this fight?

Chapter Sixteen

We pushed on up to the top of Mount Parnassus as our kernitians air-galloped along. I dared not relax for fear of falling asleep and letting go. The trees would be a hard landing in this twilight zone where the light never changed. It was dim and colorless, like the time of day back home after the sun sets, when the stars pop out. The sky's purple deepened as night claimed us again. My second one on Nostos.

Every few seconds, the fog below would clear and reveal the ground far beneath us. Cottages popped up here and there, and a dirt road snaked through the woods up and over the mountain on our left. It curved along a creek and dark things moved along it. Things with tails. The cadmean beast patrol.

Sam and Charlie rested on their kernitians, but not Leandro. He leaned forward as if urging his ride to go faster, and then a dark cloud swelled in the distance.

A swarm of black wings moved up and down. Korax—heading right for us.

"Leandro!" I called to warn him. He saw, too, and turned his kernitian down toward the treetops. Our stags followed, and I gripped the rough fur of mine as we fell through the mist that veiled my skin with a chilled glaze.

"The sky is no longer safe," Leandro said.

Neither is the ground.

Words came to me on the wind in a cackle. *Oracle. Oracle.* It echoed over across the treetops and into the purple sky, growing louder as the mass drew closer. Leandro looked at me with an expression I hadn't seen before, as if I knew what these monster birds meant by their chanting. Sam also gave me a questioning look, but there was no time to wonder.

We ducked beneath the canopy and the treetops blocked the swarm from view. We dove down fast between tree trunks, and branches stung my legs and arms as we blew past them. Leandro brought his mount to rest on the ground. We landed beside him and I eased myself off my kernitian, stiff from the long ride. We stood before Leandro, awaiting his instruction. Even Sam and Charlie were silent. We were just too tired to make a decision anymore, or rescue anyone.

"Thank you, my golden friends," Leandro said. My kernitian stamped its foot and whinnied, pushing into me with warm bristles. Then the animals departed, rising and gliding through the woods, moving their strong legs in unison as they rode the air. They soon disappeared in the unending mist.

Sam, Charlie, and I yawned at the same time. Leandro looked sharply at us. "We must go underground. And we need rest."

There was no argument with that. He swung around and strode off. None of us spoke, just followed Leandro in fuzzy obedience, hoping he would lead us to a safe, dark place to crash.

"Where are we?" I peered around in the gloom, making sure no fire-red eyes glowed back or Takers poised to jump us.

"We are just over the top of Mount Parnassus. Going down will be easier on foot. Just one Acheron creek remains between us and the bakehouse."

"What about the korax? Do you think they saw us?"

Leandro shook his head. "We only saw them because of their number." The woods grew thick and he started bushwhacking to forge a new trail. I grabbed the bushes to help, my arms aching with exhaustion, and branches pricked me awake.

"What were those birds saying?" I said.

"Oracle," Sam said.

"What's that?"

"Not what, a who," Leandro said, using his knife to chop our way to safety. "The Ancient Ones prophesied that one would be born that was mixed mortal. Part Earth, part Nostos, and part Olympian."

"Another god?" Charlie said.

"Not exactly," Sam said with a tired sigh. "This being would possess the ancient powers of all the original Olympians combined. And he would know how to re-instate the powers of the twelve gods to their heirs, and immortality would be theirs again."

"A myth some hope to be true," Leandro said between breaths. Sweat shone on his forehead and I wiped my own away, leaving behind goose bumps.

"Your myths seem awful real here," I said, tired of the history of this place where fiction came alive.

"As this one could be," Sam said, forcing a branch away, but it snapped back across his face, leaving a red welt. He rubbed his cheek, then went on. "If the Oracle brings powers to the Olympian heirs then they are called to use them for good or lose them, and the Lightning Road to Earth will be shut down forever."

"*Bonne!* A good myth to be real," Charlie said, parting leaves above his head. Leandro didn't answer and, just as I wondered where the heck he was leading us, the reason for his effort became clear. When the bush branches were parted, they revealed a tall entrance cut into rock. A cave. Leandro pulled a glass tube from his satchel and shook it. It glowed neon green like the glow sticks we got back home for trick-or-treating, only brighter. Tiny bugs ran around inside its walls.

"Cadmean beasts." Sam sniffed the air. "If we get below ground they can't track our scent as easy."

I sniffed too, but just got a whiff of wet rock and moss—no monster fox. Leandro quickly moved down into the cool blackness. Sam followed, and then Charlie, muttering about how he would not be dinner for a bunch of *stupide les renards.*

Down we went into the chilly hideaway. Leandro strode ahead, his height casting shadows from the glow stick. A musty draft wafted over me as we entered a large cavern. The walls gleamed with light in a starry dance, and soon my eyes adjusted, and the room became brighter. Pictures colored one wall in red and black with strange figures and events. My tired vision gave up trying to decipher them. Slabs stuck out from the wall, a couple of feet above the floor. I dropped down on one and its cold seeped into my bones. Water dripped in a steady beat.

"Sit down, my weary travelers," Leandro said. "It's been a while since I holed up here."

It would be nice to know when and why exactly that was, but I was too tired to ask. Charlie and Sam plopped down on slabs, too.

Charlie put his head in his hands and his shoulders shook. No words could make him feel better. Then, from under his hands, he said in a muffled voice, "How long since we left the auction pit?"

"Umm, yesterday," I guessed.

"I hope my brother was okay alone."

"I'm sure he was," I said. "He could have asked a neighbor for help or called your mom, if he knew how."

He wiped his blotchy face. "You'd be a good brother, Joshua."

"Thanks." His words made me wish harder to find Finn. As the days added up, it seemed less and less likely that we would.

Leandro pulled something from his satchel and handed us each a square bar. "This will fill you up like a meal."

I ate the granola-tasting bar greedily, sick of bong bongs and slug dogs, and gulped from the leather bag he handed me. The water tasted of honey, like the Spring of Galene.

He peered down his sharp nose at me, then pulled the bag away. "Not so fast, young Joshua. You don't want to make yourself sick." He gave me back the water and I drank slower this time.

Sam was already asleep and Charlie curled up on his side away from me, his shoulders shaking again. Then, with a final sob, he was quiet. Both he and Sam soon snored away on their slabs. Leandro plucked a thin blanket from his bag and placed it over me. He tucked it around my legs and chest, driving some of the cold away. Weariness enveloped me and my eyes closed. The last thing I felt was a rough hand on my head. It stroked my hair, and then was gone.

Chapter Seventeen

I woke up cold and sore. Charlie and Sam still slept, and at the cave entrance Leandro was spread out on the floor, his cloak wrapped around him. He breathed even and deep. Next to him, his bag rested against the cave wall that shed soft light. Now was the time to find out who he really was.

I carried his heavy bag back to my slab, wondering how he traveled with such a load, and pulled out the first thing that poked out. A book. It was wrapped in a worn leather cover and filled with stained pages of scroll-y writing. Leandro's journal. I made sure his chest rose up and down in the steady rhythm of sleep, then moved closer to the rock wall for more light and read the first entry.

History of Our People
By Leandro of the Arrow Realm, as handed down

to me by my father, Mortimer the Steel Twister

Long ago, the Greek gods fell from power. They were real and all mighty until the rise of other people questioned their rule—the Romans and then the Christians. And so, Zeus, the king of the gods, commanded his family to leave Mount Olympus and conquer a new world before their powers drained completely. They called our new world Nostos and took over rule of the primitive folk that dwelled here. On Nostos, the twelve Olympians would come to each rule a land with Zeus leading as their great king. Zeus ensured they would have a way to plunder Earth for their own use and, with his dying thunderbolt, created a Lightning Gate for each realm and a Lightning Road to travel between our lands—and between Earth and our new world. And so the Greek gods left their home, never to return or be immortal again. Or so we new people thought.

The Greek god's super powers faded forever, and over the years the powerless heirs of the original twelve Olympians squabbled amongst themselves while the lesser Greek gods blended in with the conquered people and quickly became lost in our new culture on Nostos. A select few of mixed blood held ancient powers and immortality and were forced to serve the heirs in any capacity. Many of these few came to hide their powers to remain free from enslavement. Chaos soon reigned across Nostos, and our land was plunged into the darkest of ages, leaving thousands starving and dead. The Olympian heirs believed their time had come to an end, when one discovered that mortal children of Earth had powers to fuel their world. And so began the stealing of these children for vile purposes. In time, a deep hatred of these mortals grew inside the Olympian heirs, for these Earth beings held power they now needed to survive.

Yet before this tale of woe and oppression was set in place, the Greek Ancient Ones foresaw what would become of the Olympians. Angered by the corruption their people would come to embrace, the Ancient Ones prophesied an Oracle would arise to save their world. Today the Secret Order of the Ancient Ones hides on Nostos, watching and waiting for the Oracle to come forth and redeem their people. They will protect him at any cost to save their lost world, if an immortal Ancient Evil One doesn't kill—

I flipped the page, lost in Leandro's words, when air moved across me and the book was snatched from my hands.

"What are you doing?" Leandro thundered over me, blocking out my light. He shoved the book into his bag and tossed it on the floor away from me.

"Sorry, I just want to find out who you are."

"Sneakery won't get you that. You'll know who I am when, and if, I tell you." He pulled me up, his strong hands pressing like a vise around my arms. His piercing eyes stared into mine and I leaned back, fearful he would kill me. "Don't ever go in my satchel again, Reeker. There's plenty in there to kill you with. You were afraid of the Takers? They are nothing compared to the wrath I bring."

I believed it. "Okay."

His narrowed eyes widened and he shook me loose. I staggered back and fell on my slab.

"You like to take things that aren't yours, don't you, boy?"

I shook my head and dared a glance at Sam and Charlie. Lucky them, still sleeping.

He thumped a fist to his other hand, his shape outlined against the gleaming rock walls. "You stole that lightning orb." It wasn't a question, and his fierce eyebrows furrowed in sharp lines.

I rubbed my eyes. "I borrowed it from my grandfather. He told me it had powers."

"Borrowed. Hmm. So you thought it might be useful to have on a rescue mission without knowing its purpose or the danger behind it?"

Good thing he couldn't see my cheeks burning with shame in the low light. "Why is it so dangerous?"

"It's a powerful weapon. And power in the hands of those who don't understand it is a very dangerous thing."

I sure didn't understand its power, even though driven to use it, but I kept that to myself.

Leandro crossed his arms. "So tell me, thief, why you possess ancient Olympian powers."

"You mean talking to animals? No idea. It never happened back home."

Leandro waited for more. I looked away,

uncomfortable under his gaze.

"A rare number of my people carry the ancient power of malumpus-tongue which enables them to speak to animals," Leandro said.

"Great, but why do I?"

His words cut through me. "You must be from Arrow Realm, too, Joshua."

He couldn't be right! A boy like me couldn't be connected to these Greek gods and this world. Yet, the Child Collector had smelled so familiar ...

Leandro's eyes shone in the light that glowed from the cave walls. "And only the elite Storm Masters from the Sky Realm are awarded a lightning orb upon completion of their training to serve as soldiers to King Zeus."

"But that has nothing to do with me." I pushed my hands into my thighs, wishing everything around me would disappear. "Oh, man, if we had just stayed out of the attic."

Leandro was silent, and Sam and Charlie stirred on their slabs as water trickled in a lifeless ping. "Even if you do get home, your life will never be the same again," he finally said.

The truth hit me like a fist to my gut. Nothing had changed. I was sore and tired. My friends snoozed away beside me. The water hiccupped in its endless drip. And yet something shifted in me. I *was* connected to this realm.

"Do these people steal kids for all the other Nostos lands too?" I said, wanting to change the subject.

"Yes."

"That's so wrong. I'd like to tell them that … and hit them!"

Leandro smiled, his anger with me fading. "I like your spirit, Joshua. It reminds me of someone I once knew. Someone I seek now."

"Who?"

"My wife. You see, Sam was right. I have fallen away. I'm a deserter. And I'm not a Child Collector."

He let that fact sink in for a moment.

"I was hoping you wouldn't be like the man who took me," I confessed.

"Not like him in that respect, no." He didn't share any more. "I was once a guard in the Arrow Realm at the adult work camp. It's where the mortal children from all Nostos lands are sent when they turn eighteen and lose their power. It's where I guarded those I loved." He looked away. "And it's where my wife and son disappeared."

I sat down, pulling his blanket around me, not knowing how to respond and wanting to know how he got a Child Collector's belt. But I didn't think it was the right time to ask. "What do they use kids for in your land, Leandro?"

His chin dropped to his chest. "Bait."

"Like in traps, for hunting?"

He rocked on his heels and nodded. "To hunt the big beasts of the Wild Lands."

It couldn't be true. "Do they live?"

"Not all."

"And that's okay with you?"

"It is not!" He strode to me and wrenched up his sleeve. Rough scars crisscrossed his arm. They looked like a broken arrow. I hesitated, then reached my fingers out to trace the smooth ropes that rose over his hard muscles and he flinched. "I saved many mortals from the beast hunt by chasing them into the Wild Child camp to be rescued. And I was ultimately fire-branded a failure when my arrows did not hit their targets on one hunt that Queen Artemis proclaimed 'a great celebration of our plentiful life.'"

"What were you supposed to shoot?" I pulled my hand away and crammed it back under the blanket.

He dropped his sleeve and lowered his head. His hair fell like two curtains, hiding his face. Then he sighed and bumped a fist to his chin. "Not what, who. Mortal children." Coldness soaked further into me, imagining myself being hunted by him. "I was the best huntsman there was. I provided food for my people and guarded the mortals in the work camp." His voice grew deeper. "But this I could not do."

Visions of kids being run down by arrows in a dark forest filled my head. It struck me—maybe they were the lucky ones. They wouldn't have to live anymore as slaves.

"Is that why you're helping us?" I said.

"Partly." He looked up. "I feel responsible for what my people have done to you—and continue to do. In my underground travels, I've saved a few mortal children and secretly sent them back to Earth, but that has been few and far between."

"Aren't you afraid of getting killed?"

His face crumbled. "I died long ago when my family disappeared. There is no worse death for me now."

Getting stolen away to the Lost Realm was better than the Arrow Realm. Being bait would be a way worse fate.

"We've got to stop them," I said, slapping my palm on my slab. "Get others to help. People from here or from Earth like those Takers. Why don't you do that?"

"We need a leader to rally us."

"Well, what the heck do you think you could be?" I stood up and paced along the trickling walls, unable to contain my anger at this place, these people.

"We need the Oracle."

I turned on him. "Why wait for him? He's just an excuse. I mean, kids are dying!"

Leandro stood and put a hand on my shoulder, squeezing tight. "My mission has been to find my family. I've helped mortals along the way, but I am just one soldier."

I shook his hand away. "Well, maybe you need a new mission. A bigger one, to save more than just your family."

He gripped both my shoulders this time, and his nose pressed down against mine. "You don't know our world or me. It's easy for you to judge, boy."

"I don't want to know your world," I said, slumping in his grasp as my anger faded. His did too, for he let me go, a sorrowful expression on his face.

"What's going to happen here now?" I said.

"Change is coming." He frowned, shoving his long locks back, and his thickest white streak glowed in the dim light like a beacon. "Lost Realm folk are just peasants. They fear Zeus, as well as Apollo and Hekate, and hide in their cottages, desperate for the new world their leaders have promised. To many, stealing mortals as a resource is all they've ever known. The Lost Realm may have risen out of total darkness on the sweat of mortals, but they live in a worse kind of darkness."

"What's that?"

"The darkness inside themselves."

"How do you change that?"

"Through hope, Joshua."

Chapter Eighteen

My brain burst with fantastical things, and the mysterious crude cave drawings caught my attention. Figures. Animals. Buildings. "What are these pictures?"

Leandro traced the black and red lines that swirled and looped. "Primitive drawings from ages ago."

In his tracing I saw figures walking through a giant square. "Is that—"

"A Lightning Gate. Yes. Each realm has one. It's a public way to travel between lands, and to Earth. For those with secret agendas, traveling the back roads is preferable, although more dangerous."

"Are those people from Earth?" I said, pointing at the figures.

"Could be. Our world has been plundering Earth for its own needs for a long time."

To the left of the gate was a woman in a robe. Her

hand was outstretched and something shot out of her fingers. "Hey, that can't be Hekate, can it?"

He nodded. "It may be her."

"How?"

"There are rumors that she carries the ancient power of immortality. She feeds on fear and may be an evil that's been around a long time."

A thought overcame me. "Leandro, if she's an evil immortal Ancient One, maybe a good immortal Ancient One also survived?"

"To thwart her?"

I nodded.

"You have a hopeful heart." He smiled at me. "But enough wallowing in our wonderings. Let's wake the others. It's time we moved on. We have a friend of yours to rescue."

"What if it's too late?"

Leandro placed his hand on my shoulder. His sturdy fingers warmed me. "We won't let it be."

I suddenly didn't want to leave our cold sanctuary. It was the one safe place in this dark land.

***

Charlie and Sam stirred with my shaking. They woke up, bags under their eyes reflecting the ones I probably carried as well. Our adventure was running us ragged, but Leandro paced in front of us, full of found energy.

He wasn't a man used to waiting around. He pressed energy bars in our hands and told us to eat and drink quickly.

"Leandro, what are you going do if you ever find your family?" I said, swigging from Sam's canteen.

He stopped pacing with my question. "I'll take them with me to Earth to make a new life, a safe life."

"And if you can't ever find them?"

"That thought has nearly driven me mad at times."

"But even if you do find your family, how are you going to take them to Earth?" Charlie said, plucking his teeth with a twig from his pocket.

"I have a special device," Leandro said.

"A Lightning Gate key," Sam guessed.

Leandro raised an eyebrow at him. "Yes."

"To use on the gate and get home?" *Please let it be true.*

"Yes."

Charlie frowned. "So let's go home! What are we waiting for? And why didn't you tell us you already had a key when Prince-man mentioned needing one?" He pulled his twig out of his teeth and pointed it accusingly at Leandro, who stepped toward him with a fierce look. Charlie dropped the stick and moved his lips as if trying to form words, but then coughed twice and hung his head.

"I don't have the codes to get to Earth, only to travel between realms," Leandro said, confirming what Sam had said earlier. "And I didn't know you boys well enough to trust you." Leandro gave me a knowing look. "You may have stolen it."

"Do you trust us now?" Sam said.

Even though he had saved us—even though I *felt* his trustworthiness—he was still a man with secrets. And I was quickly learning the power of knowing who and when to trust.

"Trust is earned," he said, still staring at me, and I was thankful once again for the low light that hid my burning cheeks.

"We need to earn it from you, too," I dared to say.

His brows pulled in, and he spoke in a flat voice. "I saved your life. I think you have."

"Show us the gate key," Sam said.

Leandro pulled his satchel from under his cloak and lifted out a flat square that gleamed bronze. He set it on a slab nearby and pushed at its flat surface. In an instant, the paper-thin sheet popped up into a wooden cube the size of a tissue box. Gold sparkles moved through it. In the gold flickered colored squares of rubies and emeralds like a sun in the dark cave.

"Leandro told me he's not a Child Collector," I said, confused. "And, Sam, you told us only a Child Collector carries a Lightning Gate key."

Sam flashed Leandro a sharp look but didn't speak.

"That's true," Leandro agreed. "Each Child Collector from every Nostos land has a gate key and a scroll of all the codes to travel between all lands and Earth. Only Zeus has the original code scroll to re-create the scrolls from. It's guarded well."

The golden box shimmered and pulsed. "How did

you get this key?" I said.

"I broke into the house of a Child Collector in another land and stole it," Leandro said.

"How did you get away with it?"

Leandro finally looked away from the Lightning Gate key to stare at me. "I slit his throat. But not before he gave me this." He traced the scar on his face. Charlie gasped.

Leandro held my gaze, challenging me to judge him as a thick gob stuck in my throat. It burned going down, carrying my fear with it. I hoped he never needed something from me that I wouldn't give him. "So this is how you move between these lands? By pretending to be a Child Collector?"

"Yes. It's a good cover and better than taking the back roads, which I do only when necessary. I've been attacked far too many times to make it a permanent way of travel."

"Didn't you steal the codes too? Why do you need us?" I said.

"The code set was damaged in my fight with the Child Collector, and the Earth code was destroyed. I've been attempting to steal a new set of codes for some time." Leandro held the box out toward me. "Touch it, Joshua. See how the power feels."

I pressed ever so slightly on the golden box. Heat pierced my fingertips, but it didn't burn. Tiny writing wrapped around the edge of the box. Leandro read it. "For whoso travels with the power of my lightning, must bow in my honor or face banishment and the labors of arduous journeys to come." He paused then said, "It's signed by Zeus, king of the gods."

The power of Zeus filled me, but I pulled my fingers back.

"Power. Like in you, Joshua." Leandro flattened the box, and slid it away. The gold disappeared. "Time to go, boys."

And with that, powered by strange food, sleep, and a sliver of hope, we went out again into this other world where the misty blue sun rose on another new day.

Chapter Nineteen

We were determined to keep away from the main village of the Lost Realm and trotted in single file through the thick woods. The trees pressed up against me. Their branches snagged my clothes and scratched my hands, blood oozing from tiny cuts. I wiped it away and focused on Leandro's back ahead of us.

The never-ending quiet consumed me. It was more quiet than even the mountain where Bo Chez took me camping a few times. Even in that peaceful place eagles shrieked, hikers chatted on the trails, music floated to our campsite, chainsaws buzzed cutting wood, and campers came and went on vacation in their cars. Here, no animals chattered or birds sang. Here, the quiet was dead.

Leandro stopped suddenly and put up his hand, holding us off in silence while he scanned the area. He pointed, and we followed his finger to see a cottage, camouflaged amongst the trees. Smoke drifted from its chimney. He motioned us to crouch down behind a bush.

Humming burst through the silence as a woman came out of a door on the side with her back to us. She carried a basket with lumps of white to a canopy, and began hanging up clothes on a line under it, her dark blond hair falling in waves down her back over a long aproned dress. She tapped a foot to her song that filled the air with merry cheer in contrast with the gloomy land she lived in. Leandro drew in a sharp breath. He stood up. *What was he doing?*

Sam, Charlie, and I shrugged at one another. My calves cramped up, but I held my position, breathing shallow.

"Could it be?" Leandro whispered.

As if she heard him, the woman stopped her work and turned to the side. My neck stiffened, and my eyes hurt to stare at her without blinking. *Don't see us!* Leandro's shoulders fell and he squatted down again.

"It's not her," he said.

"Who?" I whispered.

"My wife. It's been so long. I thought I would know her the moment I saw her again. I don't want to forget what she looks like."

I didn't know what to say, and Sam and Charlie didn't either as they remained silent. Leandro's task of finding his family weighed heavy in the air.

We waited until she went back inside and then we crept away from the cottage. None of us spoke for quite some time until we stopped for a drink at a tiny burbling spring and Leandro and Sam filled up their water containers.

"Who was your wife, Leandro?" I said as we continued on and navigated around a tight cluster of trees.

He didn't answer at first then said quietly, "She was a mortal in the adult camp, having been taken from Earth as a child, and held as our captive. But we fell in love and married ourselves in secret." He paused and sighed. "Her name was DeeDee."

"What happened to her?"

"She was taken away, along with our baby son, as punishment for my involvement with a mortal."

"Where could they be?"

"I don't know. I deserted my post to travel from land to land to find them."

He was so determined. With danger at every turn, how long could I continue searching for Finn?

"What's your son's name?" I said.

Leandro slowed and then stopped, looking up into the purple sky. Charlie took the stop as a sign to throw himself down on the ground, and I was thrilled for another break.

"Evander," Leandro finally said. "He had hair so blond it was almost white and a birthmark on his forearm like a flame, the noble ancestral mark of the hunters of Arrow Realm." He turned and looked at my arm as if expecting that birthmark to appear, at my hair as if my boring dirty blond would suddenly bleach white. "He would be a year or so older than you."

He pulled a miniature bow from his satchel a third of the size of his own bow.

"I made this for my son before he was born," Leandro said, running his fingers over its polished arcs. "I had hoped to give it to him when I found him." He slid the bow away.

I clenched my jaw, biting my lip by accident. Blood and pain welled. What if I couldn't find Finn, like Leandro couldn't find his son? Failure was not an option, or staying here for years and never seeing my friend again, fighting for survival, or forgetting what Finn looked like—and Bo Chez.

Leandro said no more, and we took off once again with me in front, leading the way as if I knew where to go.

***

It wasn't long before the delicious smells of fresh baked bread, roasting meat, and gooey desserts filled my nose. A crooked, black building stuck out from the mist and smoke sputtered thick at the top of its several chimneys. We'd reached the bakehouse.

I looked at Sam. "How are we going to get in there and search for Finn?"

"I know where the hidden tunnel entrance is," Sam said.

"I'm going with you."

Sam cocked his head as if wondering if that was such a good idea then he said, "This way."

"Wait, what if we're seen?" I said.

"I'm the king's son. No one questions me. The servants may not know I'm wanted yet. They certainly won't know you; and besides, the boys and girls working in the bakehouse pit are half awake, cooking the king's breakfast. They deliver it by tunnel to the castle on powered carts."

Carts we power.

"We'll wait here for you," Leandro said.

Sam pointed. "The old tunnel entrance is just past that rock."

Charlie seemed unsure about us leaving him with Leandro. "How are we going to know if anything's wrong, Prince-man?"

"You'll know if something goes wrong," Sam said. "An alarm will sound."

"I'll call the kernitians to come fly us out of here," Leandro said. "Let's hope they'll help again."

"Come back in one piece, please, *mon ami*?" Charlie looked at me and sagged his shoulders, shifting about on his feet.

I nodded, and then Sam bent down and moved some brush aside. Beneath it was a rusty round cover that blended into the earth. Sam pulled it up by a hook. Rungs set into the side of the circular shaft led down into blackness. Sam climbed down and I followed into the stuffy dark, peering one last time up from the black hole. Leandro stood expressionless, watching.

"Be safe," Charlie called. "*Au revoir.*"

***

The blue glow of the lightning orb provided enough light for us to run through the cool tunnel. Squeaks sent shivers up my spine. Monster rats or some new monster? We ran faster. Finally, we came to a solid wall and stopped. The wall had a door—we had arrived.

"Don't speak," Sam instructed. "Just follow my lead." He lifted the latch and pushed open the door. The scent of sausages attacked my nose and my stomach shriveled. We'd entered a room with shelves piled high with bags of flour, jars of strange things, and vegetables.

We tiptoed through the storage room toward light and noise as heat from the kitchen warmed my face. Ahead of us dishes clattered, pots banged, and kids jabbered. Breakfast was in progress. I was crazed with hunger for a real meal and could barely think. Sam was better off—he nabbed two white aprons from hooks, and we hunkered down in a corner behind a pallet of flour and put them on.

"The bake servants may think we work here, too," Sam said. "I just don't want to run into the head chef. He knows me."

He took something that looked like a pumpkin and

I grabbed a bag of potatoes, yearning for mashed ones with gravy.

"Act like you've got somewhere to go," Sam said.

Man, did I have somewhere to go, but it wasn't in here. Boys and girls in white aprons bustled around the kitchen. Soon we were among them in the hot room where fires blazed in hearths that held meaty birds roasting on spits, their juices sizzling on burning logs. The heat felt good at first, compared to the damp tunnel but then became sweltering.

"See your friend?"

No such luck. Sam grabbed one of the bake kids, a tall girl with chopped short hair. "Hey, any new boys come in here lately?"

The girl shook him off. "Not since two weeks ago." She ran off carrying a smoking dish of bacon. My stomach lurched in response. My last hot breakfast was days ago.

Sam ducked behind a curtain and pulled me with him. "The head chef," he whispered.

We were inside another storage area. The curtain didn't go all the way to the floor. Skinny legs ran about in the kitchen except for the fat, bowlegged ones heading straight toward our hiding place. We gripped our food. Drops of sweat rolled down the side of my face and I swiped at it with my arm. Light burst bright before us as the curtains were flung open.

"Aha!" The fat chef glared down at us with a red face. "I just heard there were outsiders in here. Thieves! And you, Sam, a traitor. Hekate wants you for questioning. You better turn yourself in. She may be the one we all answer to soon enough if she delivers on her promise." He tried to seize us, but Sam threw his pumpkin at the chef's stomach so hard that he fell on his butt. Sam ran past him with me right behind. As the chef struggled to rise, I dumped my bag of potatoes on him, sending him back down. Chubby hands clawed at me, but I pushed him away and ran past as fast as my aching legs would go.

The bake kids looked on in surprise as we flew by them back to the tunnel, but no one tried to stop us. The girl with the chopped off hair stared at me, then gave me a slight nod as if saying 'good luck.' I looked behind me once to see the chef scramble up, only to roll on a potato and fall on his butt again. It would be funny if the terror of being caught wasn't at our heels. I pulled out the orb, ready to battle. A bell gonged.

"Joshua, catch!" Sam stole a hunk of steaming meat off a platter and threw it at me. *Nothing to lose now.* The slippery mass warmed my chest with its tempting juices. Sam grabbed a loaf of bread and a pie, balancing it as he ran. We tore through the first storage room and re-entered the cool tunnel. The orb lit the way.

Faster we ran while the greasy meat tormented me with its smell, but we couldn't stop. The bell screamed out our crime. *Please let us get back to Leandro and Charlie.*

Shouts burst from behind us. My legs couldn't move any faster and my chest felt cracked in two as my lungs ached with their effort. Finally, Sam pulled himself up the rungs to the world above.

He pushed up on the hatch door. "It won't open!"

The thumping of feet behind us vibrated the rungs my shaking hands clung to in desperation. "Hurry, Sam!"

"Got you, Reekers!" Guards stood a few feet away from us, torches in hand. One held something else as well. A vape. Pointed right at us. Hissing angrily.

We were done for.

Chapter Twenty

Light splashed from above. Leandro hauled us out and slammed the hatch back down, turning the handle tight. The guards banged on it, yelling.

"Run!" Leandro pulled us toward the waiting kernitians.

"Finn?" Charlie clutched me.

"No! Just run!"

The cover to the tunnel shook with angry thumps. Muffled voices protested below. We leapt onto the kernitians and galloped into the air.

Higher. Higher.

The meat spread a greasy stain on my apron. Up to the trees we raced, and once we reached the tops, the kernitians slowed to a trot. The heat of the bakehouse left me as a soft breeze tickled my skin, and I breathed cold, soothing air.

Sam ripped off a piece of bread, threw it at Charlie,

and dug into the pie. "Finn wasn't there, but we got food!"

Leandro laughed. "By the gods! Good thinking, boys."

About time this meat was mine. I pulled off a chunk and threw it to Leandro. We tore into the food like a Thanksgiving feast and forgot about scary creatures attacking us and guards vaporizing us with snake heads. There was only good food going down into our empty stomachs. Poor Lo Chez couldn't eat any of it.

"The best agrius beast there is," Sam mumbled, his mouth full of food, pointing at the mystery meat.

Whatever agrius beast was, it sure tasted good. Better than gurgle soup. We ate until it was all gone, passing food back and forth in the sky. Charlie let out a huge burp that startled his kernitian, and it kicked its legs up. We all laughed, and even Leandro chuckled with his deep rumble. With our stomachs full, we glided along as if on a summer afternoon bike ride, except there was no yellow sun here to warm us, only a blue, frosted one.

"So, where to next?" I said to Sam.

"The castle. And the greenhouse is on its grounds. It's not far, but our most dangerous stop. The Lost Realm guards have been training extra slaves to guard the king, and Finn might be one of those. The king has been paranoid about a takeover, and if that were to happen, my days would be numbered here, which is why I needed to escape now."

"Then the rumors are true," Leandro said.

"What rumors?" Charlie said.

"Hekate's plan to overthrow King Apollo. And the people of the Lost Realm are ready for change."

"Even an evil one?" I shook my head.

"The Lost Realm is cursed, first by Zeus and now Hekate, and could soon be plummeted into the darkest of ages again," Leandro said, spreading a hand out across the treetops. "You can already feel the chill in the air and inside folks."

"Even my father is afraid," Sam said. "It's why he's had me working at the power mill and sending back reports. He was once a reasonable man, but now I fear him as much as I do Hekate."

"Because she's an immortal evil?" Leandro said.

"How do you know that?" Sam said.

"As a prison guard, I heard things."

"It's true," Sam said softly.

"Those old cave drawings looked like her," I said. "But how can you know for sure?"

"I watched her," Sam said. "One night, I snuck outside her sleeping quarters and spied her through the keyhole. She removed her beauty and there was the ugly, old hag beneath." He shuddered as if haunted by that vision. "I knew then, if I wanted to live, I had to do whatever she told me."

We were all silent for a long moment. The memory of her fingertips silencing Lo Chez with blue fire filled my head. "She doesn't need a vape, does she? She *is* a vape."

Sam nodded solemnly. "The most deadly vape of all."

My kernitian suddenly dove down, and cold air rushed over me as it zoomed toward the ground. "What's happening?"

The others dove as well. Leandro wiped the back of his hand across his mouth. "I'm not asking them to do this."

We landed on the forest floor and dismounted as whinnying came from far beyond the trees.

Leandro translated for everyone. "They've signaled danger among themselves and are calling all to return to home."

My kernitian took off like a racehorse into the air with the others. Within seconds, they were gone from view. We stood, fog rolling around our feet in a blanket that offered no comfort.

Leandro pulled out his knife. It shone in the mist. "We've got to get under cover inside the castle to find Finn. Quickly."

Sam shook his head. "There's no way in except through the castle gate, which is nearby at the edge of the woods. All the underground tunnels have been blocked off, except the other bakehouse one that leads directly into the castle."

"You already got chased out of there," Charlie said.

"Then let's take the road." I pointed through the trees at the path that wound through the woods in the distance. We'd come upon it earlier and kept it in sight to maintain direction, watchful for unfriendly riders on it.

"We'll be caught for sure," Sam said.

"I have to agree," Leandro said. "Too risky. We must find a way in through the castle's bowels."

"They wouldn't be expecting us on the road though," I said.

Charlie waved his hands in the air. "*Zut Alors!* So what do you suggest we do, Joshua? March on up, give a good knock, and say *'Allo!* We need to rescue a kid in there. Send him out so we can escape. And by the way, sorry about stealing your breakfast.'"

Something dawned on me, and I nodded. "That's exactly what we do."

Sam, Charlie, and Leandro looked at each other, and their faces told me I was crazy.

"Leandro, you pretend you're a Child Collector delivering some Reekers to the king as slaves," I said, speaking faster with excitement, knowing this would work, would have to work. "You have a belt and gate key that proves it."

He thought about it, and then a half-smile crossed his face and he shot a finger at me. "Good thinking, Joshua! You boys will be my captives."

"What if something goes wrong? We need the gate key to get to Earth," Sam said.

"And we will," Leandro said.

We stood there, no one speaking, and finally I said to Sam, "We have to trust each other."

"*Oui*, Prince-man. Trust. It's all we got," Charlie said with a serious look on his face.

At last, Sam nodded and Leandro took charge. "Once we get in the castle, we'll find Finn, get the gate codes, use the orb to blast our way out, and with the element of surprise, run like the wind to the Lightning Gate. I know the way."

"Me too, but I can't go in the castle," Sam said. "Everyone knows me. But I can tell you where the codes are."

"Wait in the woods for us then," I said.

A rush of anticipated success filled me with the bigger picture of our mission. "What about the others?" I looked at Leandro. Charlie and Sam both appeared puzzled. I explained. "Rescuing all the kids stuck here."

"First we must get your friend, young Joshua." Leandro said. "There's no time to waste."

He was right. We ran after him. This time, we had energy to burn. And it wasn't far. We ran around rocks, over water holes with scaly things flopping in their murky depths, and under the drooping wizard trees. They looked tired and sad to me now, bearing witness to our adventure unfolding. Then we stopped. We could go no further.

A raging creek roared across our path and there was no way around it. We had to cross. Tusks poked up through the churning waters.

Hydriads.

Chapter Twenty-One

Water tumbled past us in a mad flood, angry as it raced to its final destination. Two fat boulders sat in the middle of the creek.

Charlie looked around. "There must be a bridge not far from the path."

"It's further downstream," Sam said.

"And we're here now," Leandro said.

"There." I pointed. "We can jump across."

Leandro agreed, but Charlie backed up. "These ... things will get us like Leandro said."

"Not if we don't fall in," I said.

Tusks sailed back and forth in the turbulence like sharks under the water, cruising the creek floor for their next meal. They swam in wait for victims like us.

"They seem hungry," Sam said, tensing his shoulders.

"What if we do fall in?" Charlie's eyes darted back

and forth between the monster fish.

There was no answer to that.

"I'm not afraid of hydriads." Leandro pulled out his knife. "I'll slice their tusks off before they get you."

I wasn't sure if he could be that quick, but we had to cross. Vapor lay heavy on the water, hiding the full horror of what swam beneath.

"Follow me," Leandro said. "I'll go first and get you each across, one at a time."

He leapt from the bank to the first boulder. It was wide enough at the top for two. Spray jetted up, wetting his cloak. He steadied himself on the rock, then reached out his hand. Watching the tusks circle his boulder, I went first and backed up a few steps, took a running start, and jumped, landing hard. Leandro steadied me. The water banged against the boulder, as if it too wanted to pull us in.

It got its chance. I lost my balance following Leandro to the next boulder, and one foot slipped into the cold water. The tusks headed for me and something rammed against my shoe. A snout quivered above the water. Sam and Charlie yelled at me to get up on the rock.

Leandro hoisted me up just before a tusk lanced my leg. "Come now, Joshua, we can make the last leap together." Could my shaking legs make it? But he took my hand in his rough one and we sailed through the air to land on the muddy bank.

Safe.

Leandro leapt back across the creek to help the

others. First Sam came across, then Charlie. He flew through the air, his face scrunched up in terror and his skinny arms and legs spewing in all directions.

Then he missed.

He hit the last boulder off center and dropped up to his hips into the seething foam.

"Leandro!" Sam and I both yelled at the same time. Leandro looked back as he soared onto the bank ahead of Charlie. He slammed into the ground in front of us, then dashed back into the creek, and I followed. His cloak flew behind him like a flame as tusks raced toward Charlie. Leandro waded through the waves with me right behind, and we pulled Charlie up with one hand while Leandro sliced through the water with his knife.

"Joshua, part the waters," Leandro commanded.

"I can't—"

"Try!"

I pushed the waves aside, not sure how to do what Leandro wanted me to do, but the water held me greedily in its arctic grasp. Sam yelled something, but the water was a roar. Its icy spray shocked me, blasting up my nose and in my mouth with a salty, foul taste. I forced the water away, but couldn't move faster through it.

"Believe it, Joshua," Leandro yelled. You can do it!"

But I couldn't.

The water dragged me down into its glacial realm. A tusk raced toward me. Sam yelled louder. Brackish water filled my mouth, and I began to slip under.

Leandro pushed Charlie toward the bank, then swung around and hoisted me up. He flung himself about in the freezing water as tusks encircled us, moving like a boxer to dodge the spears his enemy launched at him.

Slice. Slice.

The foam bled red. Then the tusks were gone. Leandro hauled me through the water toward Charlie and Sam. We climbed up on the bank, dripping. His hair glistened against his cloak that now hung heavy on him, and he hurled down seven tusks. Sliced, jagged, and bloody.

I shivered in wet clothes, gasping for breath, and never so glad to be back on land in all my life.

Chapter Twenty-Two

We stood dripping on the mossy ground, recovering from the hydriads' attack.

"*Sensationnel*," Charlie said in a shaky voice and pushed his wet hair off his forehead in spikes.

"Not the word I'd use," I said.

"It means 'wow' to you Americans," Charlie said tightly.

"*Sensationnel* all right. Or more like—"

Leandro cut me off, pushing his face into mine. "Joshua, you can't command water."

"N-no," I stammered, my heart still knocking about in my chest. The slimy feel in my mouth made me gag, and I spat to get the taste out, but it stuck to my tongue.

His breaths slowed and his shoulders caved in. "I'm sorry. I almost got you killed. I'd hoped you'd have Poseidon's ancient power ... and be the one."

The one *what*? I'd let Leandro down, but didn't understand how. Sam wouldn't look at me, as if he didn't want to explain. I shook all over, my fingers white with cold, and stuck them under my armpits.

"Poseidon the sea god?" I racked my brain for facts on Poseidon.

"Yes," Leandro said. "He was god of many things, but he was most known as the Olympian god of the seas, protector and commander of all waters and its creatures. His heir rules the Sea Realm."

"Wasn't he Zeus's brother?" Mythology class quickly came back to me.

"Yes, and to Hades, god of the Underworld. But Poseidon fought often with his brothers, and it was said that you didn't want to cross him, as he could wreak destruction through his earthquakes and tidal waves."

"A real nice god," Charlie said, rolling his eyes with a snort as he resorted back to knuckle chewing, taking turns with them.

"Well, he is long gone and now his heir, King Poseidon, seeks out those with ancient powers. He trains them as soldiers to enforce his laws and battle anyone who defies him. Just like Zeus. Just like Artemis. It's why, being a malumpus-tongue, I was drafted as a guard and hunter to lure the beasts to their death." Leandro paced angrily before us, shaking out his wet hair and cloak and muttering to himself. "Powerless gods. They force those who exhibit the ancient powers to be servants for life. They act as absolute rulers when they should be pooling the resources of their own and raising them up to live a better life." He punched his fist into his palm, then said with renewed force, "It's time."

"Time for what?" I wrung out my sopping wet shirt and squirmed in jeans that clung uncomfortably.

"Time for our world to be redeemed, and someone must rise up to lead us." He stopped pacing and looked at me with eyebrows drawn together. "I wanted to believe you were that redeemer—and help me find my family."

Was that the only reason he stuck around? He gazed off into the woods, his mouth in a hard line. His disappointment about who I was weighed on me. I sat down and hugged my knees to draw some warmth into my body, and Sam knelt down beside me.

"I never knew if the myth was true before," Sam said, tapping his hands on his knees.

"What myth?" I said.

"The Oracle," Sam said, and stopped tapping, his fingers now bunching up his pants.

That's what the korax chanted.

Charlie spouted out a squeaky laugh. "*C'est quoi?*"

Leandro strode to me and grabbed my hand, pulling me up, his fingers covering mine. "Do you have any marks that might reveal you're the prophesied one?"

I snatched my hand away and took a step back, tripping on a root. He reached out to steady me, but I shoved him off. The waters, the animals, the eyes of my friends, and even the nearby trees seemed to want something from me. "I don't have any mark!"

"What are you saying? Joshua is some kind of Olympian god?" Charlie looked me up and down as if I were about to start spitting light from my fingers like Hekate.

Leandro paced back and forth like a caged animal, his boots snapping dead branches as he stirred up the fog in angry wisps. "Joshua here has the ancient Arrow Realm power of malumpus-tongue to speak to animals. And he has a lightning orb from Sky Realm, which could provide him with other powers here. These things add up." He stopped pacing and thrust his hand out, serving me up. "Yes, Joshua may be the Oracle destined to bring back Olympian powers to their heirs, restore right on our world, and shut down the Lightning Road forever. Every one hundred years one is prophesied to arise … if he is found."

My scalp prickled and I inhaled sharply, glancing at Charlie. His knuckle was frozen in his mouth as he stared at me. I just shook my head back and forth, wishing their stares away, wishing I could melt away in the mist and just be anonymous Joshua again in a world that made sense. Back home, in each new town, I was the invisible kid who blended in. Here, in taking risks, I was noticed at every painful moment.

"But Joshua can't command water like people from the Sea Realm," Sam said in a quiet voice, his eyes like huge black pools.

"No." Leandro's hand fell to his side and his face

sagged. "You are right. He must not be what I hoped for—we hoped for. And who knows what chance the Oracle would have here now ... "

Sam stood and pulled out a piece of wood the size of a small book from his deep pants pocket. Looking more closely, I saw it wasn't a book but wooden tubes ranging from short to tall and all bound together in a musical instrument.

"Some Lost Realm people have other rare ancient talents of Apollo," Sam said. "Like music. This pan flute is the one reminder I have of my mother. She used to play so beautifully. I'd do anything to hear it again. If only ... "

"If only what?"

"If only I'd inherited my mother's talent." He put the instrument to his lips and blew a horrid squeak that rattled my insides. Then he handed me the flute. "It seems part of you is from this world. Would you just try?"

He seemed so sad there was no way to tell him that I couldn't play an instrument. Maybe my equally awful squawk would lighten the moment.

So, for Sam—and for Charlie's continued entertainment—I took the flute and blew across its tubes. No one was more surprised than me when a melody flew out. A new force filled me up and pushed my fear and anxiety away. My lips raced back and forth on the smooth wood, changing the pitch, playing an unfamiliar song. Yellow butterflies floated down through the mist. One landed on the flute, and I quickly handed it back at Sam, who had a tear running down his face.

"You called to them, Joshua. They hide in the treetops. They only come out when a flute player calls them. Like my mom could."

"Perhaps you have two relatives from different Nostos realms, Joshua. The Lost Realm and the Arrow Realm," Leandro said. "They could have carried both their land's ancient power and passed them on to you. Your grandfather has some connection to our world. It seems you do, too." Then he added in a more serious tone. "And I would keep that a secret here."

"Why?" I said.

"If Hekate finds out, she may target you for more than an energy slave. She may want to use your double power for evil."

Sam nodded. "She thrives on power, hers and others."

Power didn't call me. Home did. And that brought with it a memory. "When the Child Collector took me, he smelled familiar, and I don't know why."

"Maybe he tried to take you as a young child and you don't remember," Sam said.

My heart seemed to clench itself and release with Sam's words. If the Child Collector had tried to kidnap me before, then why didn't he succeed?

We needed to move on, but all this information swelled in my head and I still needed more to survive here. "I bet you're sorry for following me, right, Charlie?" I said, banging a fist to a tree trunk so hard its bark chipped off.

"*Non.*" He shook his head fast, black bangs flopping back and forth. "I could have died in that pit or at the power mill. You got me out of there. Like some kind of hero. The only one I'm a hero to is my brother. Everyone else thinks I'm uncool."

"Not me."

"Yeah, well even my dad doesn't think I'm cool." He picked at a hole in his shirt.

"You faced all this danger to get back to your brother. That's heroic and pretty cool. Your dad would think so."

He shook his head again and looked at his feet, but a smile flickered across his face, and all those times I'd wanted so badly to fit in with the cool kids didn't seem important. Being kind and a good friend and a good brother was way more cool.

And with that thought, something else occurred to me. "Leandro, your wife was from Earth, so your son could be the Oracle."

He inhaled sharply. "I've carried that hope in my heart, and along with it the belief that someone powerful sensed he was the Oracle and took him, to use him or … "

"To stop him?" Sam said.

Leandro swallowed hard with a small nod. "Someone who didn't want the gods to have their power back."

"Like Hekate?" I said.

"Yes. Someone like her wants all the power for

herself." And fear filled me in knowing that having such abilities not only came with great power, but with great duty and danger. "No Oracles have been recorded in history. I suspect there were some, but they, too, disappeared. Perhaps by a royal."

"Why?" I looked at Leandro.

"Royalty doesn't want competition; royalty wants power—like Hekate. Or the Nostos rulers. They may think the Oracle will take over all Nostos and not bring back their ancestors' powers."

Sam nodded in agreement. "Kings like to control their legacy. King Apollo banished my mother to Earth for not producing an heir. Her first baby died when it was still in the crib, and he didn't realize she was already pregnant with me. She gave me a better life on Earth for six years until a Child Collector stole me. My royal lineage was discovered then"—Sam rolled up his sleeve and revealed a sun tattoo with a fancy 'A' in the middle of it on the inside of his wrist, his sun a brilliant yellow to my black one—"and I was sent to the castle to be raised with the other royal children. Not so the king and I could be reunited, but because I belonged to him. They never did find my mother, so he took his anger out on me. Since being raised amongst Reekers, I've been a disgrace to the family."

He jerked his sleeve down, ripping it in the process. And I realized, like all of us, he was marked, none of his family wanted him, and his mother, the one person that loved him, was missing.

"This world needs the Oracle," Sam said.

"Well, it's not me," I burst out.

"And be thankful about that," Leandro said in an even tone.

But even though his expectations of me quickly left, there was no going back to the old Joshua, and so the new Joshua took charge. "Time to get to the castle and find Finn. And get the Lightning Gate codes."

Chapter Twenty-Three

I pulled on the ropes binding my wrists. They were snug and scratched my skin, but there was enough room to wiggle my way out.

Leandro tugged on the cords. "Not too tight, boys?" Charlie and I both shook our heads. "Good. Now if this plan only works."

A trumpet blared through Cypress Woods, ringing like a battle cry and different from the other horn we'd heard. With that call, every sound grated on my nerves. The breeze roaring in my ears. The twigs crackling beneath my feet. And the breaths of my friends heaving in and out, like the very mountain itself was breathing us in with a great groan.

"What's happening?" The shadows revealed nothing, but grew bigger as if stalking us too.

"It's Hekate's horn," Sam said. "It always brings trouble."

"And vapes," Charlie said. "Lots of vapes."

I gulped hard, then I remembered. "In the power mill I heard her say the word 'tomorrow' to the Child Collector, like she had something planned," I said.

"And tomorrow is here," Leandro said. "Let's hope for more tomorrows." He scanned the sky that held the cold blue sun high over our heads, pale against the purple background. All of our eyes followed his, watchful for more threats, and then I looked at my friends across the blowing fog. One tall, dark, and loyal. One short, pale, and daring. One strong, battle-scarred, and determined. How did they see me?

"Sam, come with us," I urged, a growing anxiety filling me for what we were about to do.

"No. I told you I'll be recognized in the castle," Sam said.

"What if we can't get the codes?" I said.

"Do as I told you and you will."

Reluctantly, I nodded.

"Light of Sol go with you, Joshua," Sam reassured me.

"Ahh, *soliel*," Charlie said with a tired smile. "It means sun in my French."

"For us too," Sam said.

Leandro pulled us along. "Be safe, Sam."

I turned and looked back as we trotted behind Leandro toward the castle. Sam held his hand up in goodbye. Would it be the last time we saw him? The trumpet sounded again, and we ran faster. I shot a final glance back, but Sam was already gone.

***

The castle had seemed so near when its towers first poked through the treetops, but it wasn't. Charlie tripped at times, and I quickly helped him up. He shot me grateful glances as the trumpet called again but more faintly. Soon enough the woods thinned out and the road was easy to see between the trees. We stepped out on to it, the dirt hard beneath my feet after the forest moss. Out in the open I imagined fire-breathing cadmean beasts, ready to toss us up in the air as a snack.

Leandro stopped and pulled us off the road and down behind a bush. The castle stood before us, a desolate monster of crumbling torch-lit stone shrouded in mist. Its two wooden doors rose as tall as my house and a giant shield with a sun was etched into them, while a thick iron bar twisted across the sun, slicing it in two. Torches lined the front, spitting smoke that curled like fingers in the mist. Windows cut deep into the castle rock, their sightless, black holes watching us as craggy spires hovered above. The whole castle hunched over, broken and abandoned looking.

Four guards paced before giant doors with vapes held tight, pointing them outward as if expecting an attack.

"Put your heads down and don't speak," Leandro said in a low voice. His long hair grazed my face as he leaned in, smelling of pine and leather. Then he stepped out from behind a bush and tugged us out on the road. "Come along, you nasty Reekers!"

I lifted my head enough to see the guards stop pacing. They pointed their vapes at us. "Who are you, and what filth are you dragging along there?" The ugliest guard sneered at us.

"Name's Evander," Leandro said. "I'm a Child Collector from the Arrow Realm and got a request from the castle for two Reekers."

He shoved us toward the ugly guard who twitched his head at Leandro. "Show me your gate key."

Leandro pulled out the Lightning Gate key and popped it open.

"Getting a lot of these buggers in today." The guard grunted with a nod. He leaned into Leandro and spoke in a low voice. "Heard anything about a threat to the king?"

I snuck a look at the guard. His bumpy, red nose dripped with snot and I nearly choked from his stinky-meat breath.

"Only that Hekate is unhappy with the way things are going here in the Lost Realm," Leandro said, sliding his flattened gate key away and shoving me and Charlie together. Our heads cracked painfully into each other.

"Humph, aren't we all?" The guard leaned further in. "She says she can drive the mist away and bring the bright sun back to our land."

"I'm all for that. Then I won't have to grab these Reekers for a living anymore," Leandro said.

"Ha, I hear you there. Hate relying on these stinkers, eh?"

Leandro jolted our ropes hard. "That's the truth. But can Hekate do it?"

"She's wily," the guard said. "Some say she's an Ancient One with magic in her fingers. Maybe she's got a spell in there to fix things."

"Maybe."

"And there's rumors the Oracle lurks here."

Charlie and I glanced at each other. *Not me*, I mouthed.

"Eh, the Oracle is just a myth," Leandro said with a shrug.

"Hekate sensed it, they say. She would know."

"Guess we'll have to wait and see."

The guard clapped Leandro on the shoulder with a great snort and turned to the other guards. "Open the gates, boys. Another two for the king."

The gates creaked open.

"Move it, Reekers," Leandro snarled at us and yanked us along then knuckled me on the head. Did he really have to do that? He grinned out of the corner of his mouth, obviously enjoying this.

"Stupid Reekers, aren't they?" The red-nose guard roared with laughter.

"Indeed, of the most ignorant Barbaros kind," Leandro agreed.

I tilted my head as we passed into the castle to

read the large letters over the door: *To enter these doors is to gift thyself to the great King Apollo and regard him with splendor of the sun. Be steadfast in the dark and seek glory in the light that cometh soon.*

Anger boiled inside me. *Yeah, well. I'm no gift, and I'll seek glory in my own freedom, thanks very much.*

Past the guards, we entered a dimly lit hall, and the stone walls closed further in on us. Wall torches spewed smoke, and its bitterness stung my tongue when I sucked it in. With a tug, Leandro turned us around with him and called back, "I can't wait to be rid of these stinkers and get me a pint of bacon beer."

"You got that right, my friend." The guard laughed again. "When you dump them off, go find the kitchen for some. There's a pretty maid there who'll give you all you need." He winked at Leandro and they laughed together.

Then the guard pointed down the hall. "Turn right at the bend, follow that a bit, and you'll find yourself in the grand hall. King Apollo's throne is there."

Leandro nodded and pulled us along through the drafty corridor.

"We're in, boys," Leandro said, tucking the rope around his hand.

I jerked it back. "So when do I get to smack you in the head?"

"If that happens, I'll be dead and this will have all been for nothing," he said with serious humor.

"Not if you find your family first," I said.

"Yes ... but who will I be by then? And what

purpose will I have?" He said it under his breath as his feet slowed, and it seemed more like spoken thoughts to himself rather than to us, so I left it alone.

A huge clang echoed behind us as the doors slammed shut, and Leandro picked up his step again. Bolts clicked into place. Shadows loomed all around us. We were locked in.

Chapter Twenty-Four

"Joshua, keep that lightning orb on hand," Leandro said. "Surprise may save us."

I was way ahead of him on that.

We followed him past the bend. Swirly things slithered on the walls in the shadows and beady eyes followed us. I stuck close to Leandro, begging for nothing squirmy to drop down on me, when light spilled from a wide doorway before us with two guards posted at the entrance. Their vapes hissed as we approached.

One guard stepped forward. "Announce yourself."

"Evander. Child Collector with a delivery of Reekers."

The guard looked us over. I dropped my gaze to his dirty black boots. For one terrifying moment, it seemed we were done for and our lie was found out. Then he waved us in.

Leandro dragged us into the hall. A snake head lunged at me as we passed the guards. It bared its fangs and zapped out its tongue. I jumped and looked away at the brightly lit hall spread before me that was as long as the soccer field at my old school. It was a welcome warm from the dark chill we'd stepped out from, and so were the rich smells of wood smoke and roasting meat that blew over me.

We walked under giant portraits of what must have been the first Apollo: a blond giant with the sun rising bright behind him, a small harp in his hand and a bow in the other. In another he stood in a white chariot, whipping his horses on. Below the pictures, guards and boys lined the walls on both sides. Four giant chandeliers hovered with candles burning a brilliant yellow, while great logs blazed in a fireplace tall enough to stand in. A chariot covered in black grime sat like a piece of junk next to a pavilion surrounded by more guards and boys. And there, sitting on his throne, was the newest Apollo, except he was like no Olympic god I'd ever imagined. He had a pasty-potato look to him, and he spit crumbs onto his beard as he ate greedily, while servants brought him steaming platters of food.

One of those servants was Finn!

He wore a long purple shirt over gray pants and his black hair was greased back. He was alive!

"Finn," I whispered to Leandro, with a slight nod of my head toward my friend.

We reached the pavilion. The king peered down at us with beady eyes set deep in his skull. A silver crown speckled with jewels sat on his poofy white hair that glowed under a chandelier and stood out in all directions, as if he constantly pulled on it. The jewels in his crown matched the ones in the big ring on his stubby middle finger, and his square pinkie ring had the same fancy 'A' engraved on it as Sam's tattoo.

He wore a quilted purple vest and coat with yellow sunburst buttons and gold pants that bunched up around his knees while white stockings covered his legs, ending at purple boots trimmed in sparkly fringe. He reminded me of a doll in a museum. His legs barely reached the floor, and they swung back and forth like a kid at school who couldn't sit still. Around his flabby neck was a gold necklace, and hanging from it was a jeweled miniature bottle—and it contained a scroll with the Lightning Gate codes.

Finn bent over and offered him the food platter, but the king shoved it away and frowned at us as Finn looked up with a blank expression. Had they done something to him, or was I so different he didn't recognize me? I tried to loosen the ropes that scratched my wrists, eager to grab Finn and run all the way home.

Leandro bowed and motioned for us to do the same. "I bring these Reekers to you in service, Your Majesty. They will take orders and protect you."

"That one looks strong enough." The king pointed at me. "But that tall, scrawny one looks like a tiny breeze would knock him over, right Reekers?" The boys around him laughed and Finn stared at me, not at Leandro or Charlie, but me.

Leandro gave me a slight nod as he bowed again at the king. I loosened the ropes on my wrists and slipped my hands out, careful not to be seen. Charlie did the same. Candlewax dripped on the floor from the nearby chandelier like the tick tock of a clock stealing time. My fingers slid into my pocket and tightened on the lightning orb. *Finn, I'll save you!*

Then screams shattered the silence behind us as a great ringing of metal clanged. The hall door screeched open and horses thundered in. Soldiers sat high on them, swinging their swords at castle guards who chased them by horseback. The chandelier flames bent to their will. The intruders galloped the long hall toward us—and Hekate and the Child Collector led the way.

King Apollo hoisted himself up from his chair arms. The jeweled bottle swayed across his chest, the scroll inside taunting me.

Three. Giant. Steps. That's all it would take for me to rip that bottle from around his neck just like Sam told me to do. Hekate and the Child Collector stopped before the king, next to Leandro as I hid at his side.

"Call off your guards, Apollo," Hekate ordered.

The king held up his hands and the guards froze. Heavy breathing surrounded us in the sudden quiet, and the air pulsed with smoke and sweat. Swords and vapes pointed at us from all directions.

"I'd hoped for more from you, Hekate." King Apollo sighed and sank back on his chair with shaking arms.

"We could have planned something together, you and I. Instead, you attack me." His shoulders slumped. "You *are* a traitor. Like my son."

"Give it up, Apollo," Hekate said, snapping the reins of her prancing horse. "Your family lost your powers long ago. Even your son defies you."

"Your small band of loyal followers stand no chance against my soldiers," said King Apollo. A sheen of sweat popped out on his upper lip, and he wiped it away with a trembling hand.

But even as the king spoke, many of his guards, who stood beside him and lined the walls, left his side and stood behind Hekate. King Apollo rose with a fist thrust toward her, and his few remaining guards shuffled their feet, eyeing one another.

"I have your soldiers on my side now, Apollo. More will follow, along with the people of the Lost Realm, and someday all of Nostos when I claim the powers of your ancestors. You inspire no loyalty at all. You sit on your throne and do nothing, while I can deliver the sun to the Lost Realm people."

She pointed a finger at him. Blue sparks rippled along it, and Apollo flinched. "You lie, Hekate." He sat back down with a thud. "No one but the Oracle can bring back the force of the sun here."

"I can, and there will be no Oracle. I've killed every one since the gods fell." She sniffed the air, and I moved closer to Leandro who put a hand on my wrist. "And if there is a new one, I will destroy him as well." She peered around the room.

"No one will follow you," Apollo said. "You're an Ancient Evil One!"

Hekate laughed. "And you are nothing, so-called king. Admit defeat, Apollo."

"It's time for a new ruler," the Child Collector said, digging his heels into his horse. "And my sister and I are taking all the Reekers for our own use. Starting with this one." He trotted over to the pavilion and pulled Finn off it, holding him tight on his horse as Finn struggled.

"Let me smell him." Hekate leaned in and clutched Finn's shirt, her long black curls falling over his face. He pulled his head back as she breathed deep. "Nothing special here." She thrust him back into the Child Collector's arms.

"No!" I lunged toward Finn, but Leandro held me back.

All heads turned my way. The Child Collector's one eye stared into the two of mine, his charred face an angry red. "You're next, Reeker boy," he said with a snorty laugh. "And you'll find out soon enough if the cadmean beasts bite better than you."

"Ah, our little fugitives, Cronag," Hekate said, her black eyes stinging mine. "Those who escape the power mill face painful consequences. Perhaps *you* are the one I seek."

She trotted toward me on her horse, a menace whose full power I did not want to discover. A whiff of sweet roses flew up my nose as she inhaled my scent. Leandro stepped back, dragging me with him. Her eyes widened and she uncurled a crooked finger in my face—and I saw my vaporized body hanging over me—when a loud *boom* rang through the hall.

The air crackled. A ring of light whipped above us. *Blast!*

It struck the platform, splitting it in two. The king tottered on his chair and fell on his side. I lunged for him but tripped and cracked my ankle on the platform with a cry as the Child Collector's horse danced in circles. I scrambled up on the stage, barely missing a hoof to the head, and fell on King Apollo, grabbing the bottle around his neck. He struggled to get up and pushed me away, but I kneed him in the chest and tugged harder. The chain snapped. He cried out, grabbing at me, but I stumbled back with the bottle— and into the Child Collector on his horse. He snatched me up by my collar, and I kicked him hard in the leg. With an angry shout, he dropped me hard on the floor. I landed on my sore ankle and yelled in pain.

Boys ran off the platform in all directions. Hekate's horse reared up and bolted off, but she held on fiercely, shrieking. Blue fire and screams pierced the air as flames licked hungrily at the wooden stage.

A ball of ominous smoke grew behind us. Yells rang out. "What is it?" "Do you see it?"

Men and boys ran through the ash-filled air in a blur of confusing shadows. Leandro held me tight to his chest, knife drawn, and Charlie held tight to him.

"I'm getting Finn," I said, struggling against him. "We can make a run for it!"

But the Child Collector rushed past us on his horse with Finn in his grasp. Then he was gone with Finn. Again.

A figure moved confidently toward us through the smoke and chaos.

It was my grandfather.

Chapter Twenty-Five

Bo Chez flung a ball of fire over our heads. It unwound into a fiery whip. *Boom!* The air crackled again. Leandro held us back with one hand, his knife pointed at Bo Chez with the other.

I shoved his knife down. "No! It's my grandfather!"

A fiery lasso reined us in with its twisting blaze, and electricity crackled across my skin. Smoke blew thick, forcing an acrid taste in my mouth, and the shouts grew fainter. The hall vanished, and I stood in the woods alongside Leandro, Bo Chez, and Charlie. Had Bo Chez transported us from the castle to here? The towers stood faint in the distance through the trees.

Bo Chez crossed his thick arms over his wide chest, his pointy hair gleaming in the mist.

"Bo Chez!" My confusion over who he was melted away as gladness filled me, and I hugged him hard as he smiled down at me. It had to be the most wonderful, warm hug of my life. Questions wanted to burst from me, but for now I clung to his cheese and peanut butter smell, and the woods, the fog—even the very people after us—slipped away in his giant presence.

Leandro put his knife down and bowed to Bo Chez. "It's an honor to meet a Storm Master. Thanks for the rescue."

Bo Chez nodded, but his smile disappeared and he held out my arm to see my sun mark.

"Hekate branded me. It says—"

"There is no more noble a cause you bear. I know it well. Each realm has their own slave brand with an epigram that begins with these same words."

I pulled my arm away and stumbled back, twisting my sore ankle again. "Epigram?"

Bo Chez looked me up and down as if to find other marks on me. "A short phrase invented by the Greeks to inspire one to live for today because life is short."

My brain was a mix of all the events we'd survived so far, and now my grandfather's entrance and his knowledge of this world, and the homey feeling he brought with him, was fading fast. "How'd you find me?"

"Your pictures led me," Bo Chez said.

Joshua was here.

Still here.

Death was everywhere here too, and I twisted my hands in my pockets. "I got the gate codes, but we lost Finn again. They grabbed him and—"

"We'll get him, Joshua," Leandro said. "We haven't come this far to lose him. He won't be lost forever."

Like your wife and son.

I held up the tiny bottle that spun with color and freedom, and unrolled the scroll inside. It contained picture combinations for destinations to be used with the Lightning Gate key—and there was the combination to Earth.

"Put that bottle away where it's safe, Joshua," Bo Chez said quietly, and I obeyed, sliding it deep in my pants pocket. I held the fate of so many in my hands, including my own, on a quest thick with danger and destiny.

Then something occurred to me. "Wait—we don't even need the codes now, right, Bo Chez? If you made it to Nostos from Earth, then you can get us home again on the Lightning Road!"

Bo Chez shook his head. "My power to create lightning to travel—like all my powers—only works on Nostos, not Earth. And it took all my strength to use it again here. It's been a long time. Anyway, I knew you and Finn had been taken when I got home, looked for you, and found the broken window. I waited in the attic, hoping for a Child Collector to come back again for another kid. Lightning doesn't just strike once when they're involved. When one did, I forced him to bring me here. It was easy. He was a fresh recruit and terrified of me."

That was definitely not the one who stole us.

Leandro bowed to Bo Chez. "You must have been

very persuasive, sir. But what if this Child Collector talks?"

"Don't worry. He won't be doing any more talking."

Bo Chez seemed to swell bigger before me, filling my view. His muscled hands were clenched tight, and I thought about him killing a man, or cutting out his tongue, or sealing his mouth, like Lo Chez's—or maybe not even being my grandfather.

"When the Child Collector stole Finn, it was like I'd been around him before," I finally said.

"It's possible," Bo Chez said, his lips thin, holding in secrets.

"*Allons!* We need to get Prince-man, get Finn, and get back home," Charlie urged us.

A bell rang over and over in a steady rhythm.

Leandro looked at Bo Chez. "Charlie's right. We need to get the other boy first. We'll fill you in, sir, on the way."

And so we ran to find Sam.

"Wait, Bo Chez," I pulled him back. He looked at me, waiting, and so did Leandro and Charlie. Guilt burned alongside my anger, and shame, and I placed the lightning orb in his hand. It felt weird to give it back to him, as if it had become mine along the way. "Sorry I took it."

He closed his hand around it, covering it with his sturdy fingers. "I understand, Joshua." He handed it back to me. "Keep it for now. You may need it if we get separated again." He touched my head softly with his big hand, and we ran to find Sam.

Chapter Twenty-Six

Leandro neared the spot where we left Sam and motioned us down. We knelt on the forest floor, behind bushes, and the bark and pine needles poked into my pants, adding to the growing discomfort of my thirst and damp clothes. Then a horse brayed. And another. Laughter rang out, long and cruel—Hekate.

"Your friends won't recognize you now, traitor. Since you won't tell me where they've disappeared to, you can suffer in silence. You don't have long. And neither will your friends!"

Another familiar voice rang out, deep and menacing. "Serves you right." The smell of sour milk and burnt grease blew over me. We all crouched further down.

"Your father is done, like you. I've got the castle and all the workhouses now!" Hekate said.

"But, Kat, you promised me the bakehouse," the Child Collector said.

"Yes, Cronag," Hekate said in a softer voice. "If you can whip these Reekers into shape for me, you can run the bakehouse. They'll make all your favorite disgusting foods."

"And bacon beer. *Lots* of bacon beer."

"Enough! If your stench hadn't covered up his smell, I would have grabbed the Oracle sooner. We'll reorganize the workhouses soon enough and set out to conquer all of Nostos, but for now I want the Oracle. And that Storm Master is mine." More cruel laughter. "Then I'll take care of the rest of Apollo's heirs."

Hooves hammered by our hiding spot, heading away from the castle. Hekate's sickly sweet rose scent rolled by and, in the wake of the Child Collector, a putrid breeze. I peered over the top of a bush. An army of horses roared past in the forest as Hekate's soldiers followed her on a mission.

Her robe streaked behind her, a green-gold blur parading like a battle pendant. She whipped her horse on as the Child Collector oozed over his poor horse, straining to keep up. And there was the top of Finn's head.

Then they were gone. Sticks and pebbles stuck to my knees. It felt good to stand, my legs numb from kneeling on the hard ground.

"We'll get him back," Leandro said, pounding a fist on a tree trunk. "We know which way they're headed."

"We need to get Sam first." I strained to find him in the gloomy woods. Leandro pointed. Sam was curled up on the ground, facing away from us.

We all ran over and, with my hand on his shoulder, I rolled him toward me, but fell back when I saw his wrinkled face. His white hair was streaked with gray and his hands were bony with knotty knuckles and long, yellow nails. He smelled like an old book that had been closed for a long time.

I crab-walked backward fast, my hands scratching across dead bark. Leandro pulled me up, and we all stared at Sam in silence.

"What on Earth?" I said.

"This is not of Earth, Joshua," Leandro said in a low voice. "It's an Old World curse."

Sam, the old man, struggled to get up. I closed off my fear of touching him and pulled him up, supporting him under his arms.

Sam looked at me with a creased forehead. "Did you get the codes?" It came out a whispery rasp.

"Yeah."

He half-smiled, then bent over coughing. "Hekate, cursed me."

"Bo Chez, what do we do?" I said.

He thumped a fist to his jaw. "There's nothing we can do."

Leandro nodded. "There's no cure for the Old World curse. You can only slow its effects down."

"There must be a way to stop it!" I protested. Even Charlie had nothing funny to say for once.

"The one way to get rid of it is give it to someone else," Leandro said, sharing a meaningful look with Bo Chez.

"How do you do that?" I stiffened. My hands were pressed up against Sam's paper-dry skin. "Is he contagious?"

"No, but he must decide whether to pass this fatal curse on to someone else. Or he can choose to accept his own death," Leandro said. "We'll bring him with us. It's time to move now. We have the codes to get back to Earth."

"Is that all you care about, the codes? I mean, look at him!" I said, waving a hand at Sam.

"Yeah," Charlie shouted back.

Leandro's voice boomed at me. "Don't pretend that you don't want to use the codes too. If Sam is to die, at least we can save ourselves."

Leandro was right, and Charlie must have thought so, too, because he was silent.

"We now have another problem, Joshua," Leandro said. "Hekate thinks you're the Oracle."

"She does?" Bo Chez said, staring at me.

"It's dangerous for her to think so," Leandro said.

Bo Chez nodded this time, still looking at me with puzzlement.

Sam coughed again. "She'll never stop coming for you." His hair seemed grayer than it had just a moment ago. His face more lined as the curse developed with super speed.

My arms shook from holding him. Bo Chez took him from me and held him like a sick child, just like when I had strep throat and he fed me popsicles and ice cream. He sat with me for two days, telling me funny stories to ease the pain. He even slept in the armchair one night. He was no mother, no nurse, but he stayed. Soon after, I remembered wishing to be sick again so Bo Chez would be by my side night and day, just one more time.

"He's growing older by the minute," Bo Chez said.

"How long does he have?" I said.

"Days, perhaps. The young ones last longer. Unless we can find the Moria plant. It wards off death. When crushed up and placed under the victim's tongue, it slows down the advance of the spell. It could give him a few more days … or weeks."

"Otherwise Sam will die from old age?" Charlie said. It was the first time he'd ever called Sam by name.

Bo Chez nodded.

"Leandro," I said. "Where can we get this Moria plant?"

"If the Lost Realm grows any at all, we'll find it in the greenhouse."

"What about other realms? We could go there. Wouldn't one of them help?" There had to be others on this world who would come to our aid.

Leandro shook his head. "There are worse fates for you in other lands if you're caught. You could end up working with the cadmean beasts to mine coal in the Fire Realm. Or thrown in the water and chased by hydriads for fun in the River Realm races."

Or used as bait in the Arrow Realm. Staying here was way safer than any of that.

"But even if we find this plant, he'll still die?"

Please say no. But he nodded. "Then we've got to give the curse to someone else. But how?"

"Sam must cut off a lock of his hair and burn it," Leandro explained. "Then fling the ashes on the person he chooses to pass the curse on to. Only his hand can achieve it, but I don't know the spell for it."

"I do," Bo Chez said. "We had to memorize them in Storm Master training in case we ever encountered this curse weapon in warfare. It goes, 'Ashes to dust, is what's left of me. Unless, to live, I pass this to thee. Then ashes to dust now you will be.' Can you remember this, Sam?"

"I think so." His voice quavered as he repeated the spell. "I know it. It's similar to an old childhood rhyme we would sing. But—" He coughed again and couldn't stop. And I was dumbfounded by the rhyme that came to Bo Chez so easily. He had lived a whole different life before me.

Charlie spewed out a sigh. "*Mon dieu*, we've got big problems here. Bad men want to kill us. One of us needs a cane. And we're stuck on another world!"

Sam recovered from his coughing fit and motioned for me. He pressed his gnarled fingers to my arm, his brittle nails digging into my skin. "Hope."

"Hope?"

"There's a reason you came here. You could be the hope we need to change things on our world."

"*Mon dieu*," I whispered with a gulp, not wanting to be the hope for a whole world.

Then Sam closed his eyes. "Not passing the curse."

His words commanded the sudden silence, and even the breeze that chilled my skin stopped blowing as if it listened. Sam seemed even more shriveled now, and he feebly tugged his flute out and held it toward me in his shaky hand. "Joshua, take this."

"But it was your mother's," I said.

"Yours now. You can play it. And you may need it."

I ran my fingers over its smooth, worn ridges, then put it in my back pocket. What do you say when a dying friend passes on his most prized possession? "Thanks" didn't seem to cut it.

Sam went limp in Bo Chez's arms, and we were all paralyzed for a moment. Then I motioned for us to move. "Come on!"

"Joshua's right," Leandro said. "We can't stand here any longer." He plunged ahead through the fog that crept over us.

We ran after Leandro.

We would save Sam.

We would get Finn back.

We would get home.

Leandro would find his family.

We could do all this. We had to.

Chapter Twenty-Seven

We reached the same creek again. Its waters still raged around the boulders, although they now ran clear. More hydriads replaced the ones Leandro had killed. Their tusks cruised back and forth through the water as if waiting for our return. The bloody spears of their friends still lay scattered on the creek bank.

"Hekate and her army crossed here," Leandro said, searching the markings on the ground. "She didn't even take the bridge. She's not afraid of the Acheron creeks. The hydriads must fear her. I bet that evil witch is headed back to the power mill. It's her home base."

"Can we call the kernitians?"

Bo Chez stared at me. "You can speak to animals." It wasn't a question.

"I—yes."

"It's been a long time since I knew a malumpus-tongue." His face sagged, and he looked old for the first time.

I desperately wanted to know when that was but now was not the time.

Leandro and I called to the kernitians. My voice was hoarse and burned with our call for help. We waited as the sky deepened its purple, a heavier darkness creeping over me. Still nothing.

"I fear they won't come," Leandro said. "Not when an alarm has been sounded. They could be in hiding. They're timid creatures."

And they didn't.

"We have to jump across again," I said, and then Bo Chez was in the air with Sam in his arms, leaping to the first boulder. The hydriads swam faster, banging into his rock, as the frothy foam spewed salty spray at us. Charlie chewed on his fingers with renewed intensity, flicking his eyes to me and back to the watery devils.

"We can do it, Charlie," I said.

But he just stood there, gnawing on a finger.

Bo Chez was already leaping off the last boulder and onto the other side. Leandro went next. He, too, landed safely. "Charlie and Joshua! Hurry!"

I tugged Charlie's shirt and finally, with wide eyes, he took a deep breath, ran back, and jumped. His long legs made it easier for him than me. He landed steady on the first boulder, hesitated, and launched himself once more. Hydriad tusks raced around the rock in a vicious circle. He jumped again, off balance. And even before he slipped I knew he wouldn't make it. Charlie hit the boulder. He clung to the top of the rock, his left leg in the water. Tusks thrashed back and forth as he screamed.

"Charlie!" I rushed into the icy water, pushing it angrily away in my eagerness to save my friend. It stung like a thousand icicles jabbing into me.

"Joshua, no!" Bo Chez strode into the creek.

Leandro sailed through the air past him to me, and we both yanked Charlie up and pushed him toward the bank where Bo Chez dragged him to safety. Leandro and I were close behind when a great wave of water slammed into us. We fought our way against the current to get back to the creek bank when hot pain cut through me. A tusk was plunged into my side. Hot needles stabbed me. I clenched the tusk and pulled it out. It glistened red. I shoved it into the rolling water and stumbled forward against the waves.

"Joshua!" Leandro lunged for me.

Water roared down on me and all became black.

* * *

Everything was a bouncy blur. Leandro held me as he ran over rocks and logs. Ripping pain shot into my side.

"Hydriad disease." Bo Chez's words carried to me.

Charlie then spoke in a wobbly voice. "Leandro, you said the plant that can cure Prince-man may grow in the greenhouse. Can it help Joshua, too?"

Leandro held me tighter as he ran, his ragged breath on my cheek smelling of bittersweet chocolate. "It should. The Moria plant can just slow down a curse that poisons the soul, such as Sam's, but it can cure true poisons of the body."

"But you're not sure?" Charlie's voice cracked.

No one answered. Only rhythmic breathing and footfalls followed along with me now. My head was thick and my body was speared through with pain and fever, yet I shivered in wet clothes.

Leandro and Bo Chez's voices tumbled together.

"Sir, if he has Apollo's ancient power of music perhaps he could—"

"No! He is not what you want." Bo Chez's voice boomed then softened. "He's too weak, even so. The plant is our best bet."

"I am sure you're right on both accounts," Leandro said.

Moaning, I opened my eyes and tried to focus, but even the dimness of the Lost Realm burned hot in my head.

"We're almost back at the cave, Joshua," Leandro said.

Bo Chez's large hand brushed my sweaty head as he ran alongside Leandro. Even with my eyes closed I'd know his smell anywhere. It was home.

And so we returned to the cave that sheltered us before, but this time Charlie was the only kid standing.

The blurriness overtook me and, once again, darkness claimed me.

***

Cold rock against my hot skin shocked me awake. We were back in the cave. Nightmares clung to me and swirled away. Coldness filled me, although sweat lined my upper lip and Leandro's cloak lay heavy on me. Sam was under a blanket on a slab next to me, unmoving.

"Leandro, you said we can save Joshua and slow down Prince-man's curse," Charlie said. "*If* you can find the plant and *if* you come back." He sighed and muttered. "*Zut!* These 'ifs' just get more and more terrible."

Zut! I wanted to say, but my tongue wouldn't form the word.

"I'll find the plant and I'll bring it back." Leandro turned to me. His nostrils flared and, even in the low light, his eyes glinted with fierce determination.

"I'm going with you," Charlie said in a hoarse voice. Leandro looked at him for a moment, then bowed.

"My lightning will send you there," Bo Chez said.

Leandro nodded and touched Sam's head. "He's getting worse. We need to hurry." Then he bent down and inspected my wound. His rough hands were surprisingly gentle. "Joshua's wound is festering and dehydration will set in. He needs spring water." He poured it slowly in my mouth. It cooled my throat, but I was still hot one moment and shivering the next. The pain was made worse by hunger, thirst, exhaustion, and despair. After all we'd been through, we were going to fail.

I tried to speak, but the words were hard to form. Finally they came. "Save Finn."

And then I cried, something I hadn't done in a long, long time. I cried for all the circumstances that got us here and for all the things we'd suffered with no end in sight.

Leandro pressed a hand to my forehead and stroked my bangs back until I was all cried out. Bo Chez bent down to take my hand, but it was Leandro I needed. I reached out my hand to him. He glanced at Bo Chez, then took my hand, gripping it hard, his muscled fingers heavy on mine.

"Light of Sol go with you," I whispered, wanting to find hope in his world's saying.

"And you, Joshua."

Leandro moved to stand by Charlie, who gave me a brave thumbs up even as he jittered about on his feet.

"Safer to follow Leandro than me," I told Charlie.

"But you'll get me home to my brother, just like we'll get you to Finn," Charlie said with a lopsided smile.

Then Bo Chez threw his ball of fire overhead. It grew into a blazing rope winding around Leandro and Charlie and, just like that, they were gone.

I needed the truth now from Bo Chez. In the weak light, his giant shadow grew even larger on the wall behind him. He moved toward me but wouldn't meet my eyes. The damp air crawled on my skin and the water dripped in an empty rhythm. The cave walls moved in and out, threatening to swallow me. I closed my eyes. When I opened them, Bo Chez was looking at me. Then he sat down on the slab.

My voice came to me again. "One more story, Bo Chez. About you."

He nodded, and began.

Chapter Twenty-Eight

"My given name is Patrok. It means glory of the father—and I was for some time, until my father died. I got lucky with a new family when your mother and you came into my life. And I loved your mother like a daughter, Joshua." He paused and sighed. "She was mortal, but I'm not."

"What *are* you?" I could barely whisper it.

The skin wrinkled around his eyes and his massive shoulders fell. "I was a Storm Master, long ago, and came from the Sky Realm ruled by Zeus, the heir of the first Greek god Zeus." He swiped his prickly hair, exhaled deeply, then went on. "You see, the myth of the twelve Olympians is true, Joshua, but what mortals don't know is that they fell from power, lost their immortality, and left Mount Olympus to each rule lands of their own on Nostos."

Leandro's journal told me this, but the wall

between me and Bo Chez grew taller, our division stronger in knowing he wasn't from Earth.

"Did you come from a fallen god, too?" I sunk into Leandro's cloak.

"Not exactly. I'm a blend. My people come from this world Zeus took over and renamed Nostos two thousand years ago. Since then, a new people evolved over time of mixed descent."

"With your power, you must have some fallen god in you though."

"Their ancient power, anyway," Bo Chez said.

"How did you become a Storm Master?"

"My mother and father died in a war when I just turned twelve, and I became a ward of the gods. King Zeus took a liking to me, saw I carried the ancient power that only a rare few had—to command all weather—and so he drafted me into his service. I had no choice but to train as one if his elite soldiers: the Storm Masters. Our job was to protect Sky Realm, and other realms Zeus commanded to protect."

"So you were trained to zap and transport?"

"That was part of it. I mastered the art of the storm. Hurricane. Tornado. Blizzard. Ice. Rain and lightning." Bo Chez paused. "Hekate holds ancient power, too."

"But she uses her power for evil," I said.

"Yes."

"And you were given the lightning orb by Zeus?"

"Yes. All Storm Masters receive one upon graduation. They are the original orbs created by the first Zeus and passed down from generation to generation as Storm Master's retire. It's a weapon to be used with care."

"Jeez, do I know that." Dizziness flared, and the room spun like a carousel. When my head cleared I asked, "But you never used the orb on Earth?"

He knotted his hands together and lowered his head, but he didn't answer. The drip of the cave water made his silence worse. I tried another question. "And you really don't have powers on Earth like you do here?"

"I've never tried to use them there. Well, there was one time … "

"When? And why just once? Did it work?" My questions came out in one tumble.

"No, and power not used is power lost." Leandro had said the same thing … .

But he'd only answered my last question, notching up my fear. "You wanted it lost?"

He looked up. "I left my world behind for that purpose."

"So how did you end up on Earth?"

"I didn't want to be a soldier, using my storm powers to fight. I saved up my soldier's pay to bribe a Child Collector to send me to Earth when I was a young man."

"And in your stories—" Pain flared, and I clenched my teeth to go on. "*You* were the lost Storm Master, weren't you?"

He looked around the cave then back at me, his eyes crinkled at the edges. "Yes, but I never thought we'd be talking about this here."

"Did you fall in love with Zeus's daughter like in the Storm Master story you told me?" I said.

"Yes. Asteria was her name. I believed she was part of a secret order to protect the Oracle, but she would never confirm the truth. Zeus would have punished her severely if it was true because he wanted to find and control the Oracle for his own power. And Asteria's secrecy became a crack between us. I never saw her again."

My entire body ached on the cold rock. More uncomfortable was the thought of Bo Chez with a girlfriend. I shifted my legs and he put a hand on one, warming me.

"It didn't matter anyway because, like the story, Zeus demanded that Storm Masters make a vow to never marry," Bo Chez continued. "Zeus needed us to defend his land and his world. I was fine with all this until Asteria came along. She was so beautiful on the inside and out."

His face blurred. *Don't pass out!* Not when there was so much to know, just not of the yucky love stuff.

"My mother ... " I whispered.

"She showed up one day. And my life changed again," Bo Chez said.

"How?"

"Even though your mother wasn't my daughter, I became a father—and a grandfather."

"You're not my grandfather." The absolute truth of it hit me like a fist to my chest.

"Not by blood." His grip on my leg tightened as if to lessen the hurt of those words.

But I knew with certainty that I really was alone—here and on Earth.

"Tell me about her." The pain in my side throbbed painfully, but then numbness crept in.

Bo Chez stood and paced the cave wall with his hands locked behind his back, his footsteps in sync with the *drip-drip*. "She said she'd been kidnapped as a child. Like you and Finn. She grew up working in the bakehouse in the Arrow Realm. That's—"

"Where Leandro's from," I said.

"Yes, and when your mother was eighteen she was sent to the adult work camp. She didn't give me many details about that. She escaped and somehow got a ride to Earth and—"

"Leandro's wife was a prisoner there. She might have known my mother in the work camp!" I tried to sit up but the room raced around me in circles and I fell back, my heart racing.

"Maybe, we'll never know for sure. But after she escaped she arrived at my house one day, alone and very scared. We had a deep connection, both being fugitives from another world."

"And was I there?"

"No. You were born later." Bo Chez stopped pacing.

"And my father?"

"I don't know who he is. But from the way you carry ancient Olympian power, your father must be from Nostos."

But my mother wasn't, or was she? Playing Sam's flute came to me. Why did I have powers from two realms here? It was all muddled in my head, and sharing it with Bo Chez right now was too difficult.

I tried to will strength back into my body but couldn't even sit up. I pulled Leandro's cloak tighter to me, fingering its woolen warmth and closed my eyes, drifting down the muddy banks of the creek behind our house where Finn was building our fort. I waved at him, then lay back in the creek's lazy flow and began to float away … .

Bo Chez shook me. Home faded. "Wake up, Joshua. Don't go to sleep. Hang on until Leandro and Charlie get back."

I forced my eyes open. We were both quiet for a moment.

I had to know more. "Why did my mother go to your house?"

"It used to be her house. When a child returns to Earth through the Lightning Road, they return to where they left. When she got home, her family was gone. I promised to take care of her and help her find her family, but we never did."

"That's why we moved all the time—because you were looking for my mom's family?" I said.

"Yes. That, and I didn't want us to be found."

"How come I never had these powers back home, Bo Chez?"

"Yours appear to be activated here as mine are."

"But the lightning orb works there?" I said.

"Yes."

"Do other things?"

"Yes," Bo Chez said harshly, then his voice softened, and he placed a hand on the side of my head as he used to do when I was sick. "I'm sorry I made life so hard on you."

"Not so hard." It came out a whisper. All my life I'd thought Bo Chez was afraid of lightning like me, but instead he could create it. He was more powerful than lightning itself.

"I had to protect you, Joshua. I was scared someday a Child Collector would steal you. I kept moving us around and had my name changed to Cooper, your mother's name, so we could be a family. And we did become a family. Well, at least ... we were."

"We could still be." I looked at his hands that had taken care of me. Wasn't that what family did? Even if it wasn't blood family? He could have given me up for adoption, but he kept me. That counted for something.

"Did my mom really die?" Time pressed down on me as I needed the truth.

The *drip-drip* slowed as my breaths came faster, and I scraped my fingers alongside the slab, trying to hold on to it.

Finally, Bo Chez bowed his head and said the words I didn't want to hear. "Yes."

Hope fled as quickly as it came. "Because of me."

Bo Chez jerked his head up. "No. There were other ... things."

"Tell me."

Was it fever or confusion? Bo Chez's figure blurred again. *Stay awake!*

But that was it—as if Leandro's cloak had been drawn over my head, I slipped into complete darkness, half-hearing these final words: "You *are* my grandson."

Chapter Twenty-Nine

Bo Chez shook me awake as Charlie bounded into the cave, Leandro close behind.

"I've found the one Moria plant," Leandro said, catching his breath. "We broke into the greenhouse. There were only two guards out front. The majority of the army must be with Hekate."

"The kernitians finally came out of hiding. We 'hitched a ride,' as you Americans say, all the way back here," Charlie said, talking fast. "Stole some bong bongs, too." He threw a bag of them onto my slab. Bo Chez handed me one, and it took all my effort to get the dry biscuit down, but my body craved food even though my tongue tasted like sandpaper. I ate another, drank water, and fell back on the slab, buried under the cloak, only able to move now from my waist up as numbness seized my legs.

"Bo Chez," I whispered. "My legs." He squeezed

my hand. I felt like I was dying, inch-by-inch, like Sam. He was still curled up on his side, so still.

Leandro plucked a few leaves off the small plant, crushed them, and moved toward me.

"Sam," I wheezed out. "Give it to him first."

Leandro nodded and placed some under Sam's tongue then mine. It was bitter and made me gag. He then pushed some right into my wounds. I moaned, and he mumbled an apology, looking at me with concern, his fingers pressing softer on my wound. Then he plucked the few remaining leaves and hid them in his satchel.

I peered up at Leandro, my tongue thick, my question on my face.

"If it's going to work, it will do so in minutes," he said.

Seconds ticked by with the drip of the water. The fever left me with each stride of Bo Chez's pacing. My legs, once numb, prickled back to life. My foot twitched, and Charlie whooped as if I'd flown. I glanced at Sam, wanting to share this good news with him, but he didn't move.

Leandro moved toward him, knife in hand. In a slash, Leandro cut a lock of Sam's hair and placed it on a slab. Bo Chez then flicked his finger, and a spiral of light streaked out. Poof. The hair burned bright and turned to ash. Its smell lingered in the air. Leandro scooped it up and tied it in a small bag he pulled from under his cloak, then he handed it to me.

"Keep this safe for your friend."

I paused—still in awe of what Bo Chez could do—and slid the bag in my pocket as I slowly stood.

Charlie grabbed me in a hug. "Joshua!"

"You saved me," I said.

Charlie shrugged. "I just followed Leandro."

"Pretty brave and cool of you."

Charlie's face split open in a huge grin and he chewed on a finger, shifting his feet about.

With new strength, I pushed Bo Chez about the one thing he had kept from me. "Tell me now. How did my mother really die?"

His face bunched up and he twisted his hands together, then finally spoke. "I'm sorry."

"About what?" I said.

"I lied to you about your mother."

I waited, still as stone. Even Charlie stopped chewing on his finger. The *pling-pling* of the water rang in rhythm with the breaths of my friends: Sam's slow and steady, Charlie's fast and anxious, Leandro's deep and calming. And that's when Bo Chez said, "She didn't die when you were born."

My brain felt like it was being squeezed in half. "W-what?"

"You saw her die. But you wouldn't remember. You were only two," Bo Chez said.

Panic blazed through me, as if lightning had struck.

"Stop." Damp air wrapped around my throat threatening to choke me.

Bo Chez gripped my arms. "You need to know, Joshua!"

"So … dizzy." I closed my eyes.

"Hold onto me."

I squeezed his arms. "My chest hurts."

"Open your eyes, Joshua."

No!

"It's time you knew the truth."

So much had been taken from me. I couldn't stand for any more to be.

I opened my eyes, and looked at the face of the only family I'd ever known. "What did I see?"

"The Child Collector vaporizing your mother."

Charlie gasped, and Leandro growled. My hands fell away, but Bo Chez held me tighter.

The Child Collector killed my mother.

Something inside me silently broke.

I managed one word. "Why?"

"Part of a Child Collector's job is to kill escapees, but the list is long, and their resources limited. That's probably why it took so long for your mother to be found. I heard your mother scream one night. I grabbed the lightning orb and ran into her room. He stood there, laughing, his vape aimed at her. I tried to use my storm power, long abandoned, but it didn't work, and before I could throw the orb, he blasted her with you right there in the bed where she'd been sleeping next to you. And then she was gone. Like that."

The awfulness of that—for him, for me—struck hard. "I don't remember. My own mother … and I don't remember."

Bo Chez let go of my arms and nodded, along with

Charlie who was speechless for once.

"That's a blessing," Leandro said, as if he understood that loss in not remembering his wife's face. He took a quick step toward me, his jaw clenched, and his hand stretched out as if he wanted to comfort me, but then he fisted it and placed it on his knife, the blade's edge gleaming from the top of its holder.

And in that glint, a seed of memory sparked in me. A bright flash. *Zap. Zap.* I flinched as if struck.

"What's wrong?" Bo Chez said.

"It was so bright. A lightning bolt in my room. And so loud. I was so scared. There's the Child Collector's face! But where's hers?" I reached inside my pants pocket and pulled out my mother's photo, tracing her face, and Bo Chez touched mine.

"You remind me of her," he said.

I so badly wanted to remember being with her.

"That's why lightning terrifies you," he said. "I never realized … ."

Lightning took my mother from me, took my friend, and took me. But it saved my life with the orb and it brought Bo Chez here. It could bring us home.

I put her photo away, my fingers trembling with so many emotions flooding through me. "What did you do, Bo Chez?"

"I grabbed you and threw my orb at him. He blocked it with his vape, but it still sheared off half his face."

"You made him a monster."

"He already was a monster," Bo Chez said in a flat

tone, with an ugly twist to his mouth.

"Then what happened?" I said.

"He disappeared. Took the Lightning Road back, I assume. You and I left that night. If I'd gotten to your mother sooner—"

"Not your fault." I wanted to believe it, wanted to feel like he was still my grandfather, but he was a stranger now and always had been.

"We kept moving after that," Bo Chez said. "I couldn't take a chance of losing you, too."

Chapter Thirty

"**W**hat's going on?" Sam's voice rang hoarse through the cave, startling us all awake after we had finally fallen asleep once more, desperate for rest. My third night on this world. How many more would I count? Sam sat up, his face was still an old man's, but the Moria plant was working!

And then a sugary voice sent goose bumps along my arms.

"Come up, my little Reekers, I know you're down there."

"Hekate!" Sam stood onto shaky legs. I held his bony body steady as my heart hopped like a cricket.

"I'm not used to waiting." Hekate's creepy voice echoed down into our cold pit. "My army is up here. I just want the Oracle. The trail of his smell has finally betrayed him."

How could she know about me? I barely knew

about me.

Bo Chez gathered us near him. "I'm going to blast us out of here to the woods. My powers only work a certain distance the more I transport, but if we can lure them to a field I can create a storm to trap them there."

"We know you're down there, ignorant Barbaros," another hateful voice barked. "Come up now, or I'll give you a nasty bite."

Bo Chez threw his arms overhead. Fire blazed in a snake of light and lassoed us. Rock crashed down. I breathed in dust and grime, and a second of black took the world away. When it reappeared, we were crouched on the ground, back in the woods where smoke blew thick.

Charlie stood up and stumbled, but I pulled him back down. Trumpets and shouts burst out. Through the smoke, ghostly horses pawed the ground and spears poked through the mist—Hekate's army. We must have slept all night, for the dim blue sun hung over us, and the light of day made it harder to hide.

Leandro leaned in. "We've got to call the kernitians."

"But you said they wouldn't come if they fear a battle," I said.

"Everyone fears a battle, Joshua," Leandro whispered back. "But a good leader will convince his troops that when what we're fighting for is right, fear should not stop us."

I didn't know how to get home and much less

about how to save a whole world, but something in Leandro's speech inspired me. He believed I could make a difference, and in his belief, I found mine.

Bo Chez's face offered no answers. This was my decision.

I summoned what confidence I could and called the kernitians into action.

Leandro raised his head and added his voice to mine. We pleaded with them for help to win our battle. And then feet moved like wings through the air above us. The kernitians answered our call to help, and we swung up on them. Across the sneaking fog and smoke, red eyes glared at me and snarls filled the air. Our enemy found us.

"Get the Reekers!" Hekate reined in her horse and beside her, the Child Collector shook a vape at us. Bo Chez flung his hands out and sheets of rain poured down on our enemy. The soldiers' horses reared and pawed at the air as a river pushed fast behind and swept them along between the trees. They swam fast against the strong current, Hekate in the lead.

A few cadmean beasts leapt high, missing the raging torrent—but were no match for our kernitians that pushed upward as jaws lunged at our feet. Teeth, sharp as razors, snapped at me. Charlie kicked a cadmean beast in the snout. It barked in pain and fell, swirling away in the roaring water. Leandro led the way over the trees, their branches seeming to hold us up in their thorny palms, and rising up from the foggy forest the soft purple light from The Great Beyond grew before us. Below, the water receded as quickly as it came, and soldiers stampeded around trees, following Hekate's emerald streak.

Arrows shot past our heads as we moved up higher, and I dodged one just in time. Bo Chez flung his arm down, zapping bolts from his fingers. Light blazed. Screams rang out from the forest floor.

"Joshua, catch!" Leandro pulled his son's bow out of his satchel and threw it to me.

Newfound strength raced through me. The Moria plant had done its job and more. Leandro then threw a sack of arrows and it hit my chest with a *thud*.

He pulled out his bow. "Shoot, Joshua! Just pull back and aim. See?" Leandro fired more arrows. They must have found their mark because far below, guards toppled from their horses. Some got caught in their stirrups and were dragged along. They looked like toy soldiers.

"Get them good, Joshua!" Charlie said, his eyes round with fear.

I had never used a bow and arrow in my life, but found myself calmly putting an arrow to my bow and aiming it at the enemy below.

"Now, Joshua!" cried Leandro. I drew back the bow with steady fingers, my arms burning with the effort, and picked a point ahead of the army—then released the arrow. It sped off like a rocket and struck a cadmean beast. The beast shrieked, smashed into a tree, and lay still. My heart raced as I drew back another arrow, and another, alongside Leandro. Two bows, working together. One giant, one not-so-grown-up-sized.

Leandro turned to throw me more arrows when a spear of blue light pierced my hand. Sparks ripped across my fingers. Pain launched through me, and I screamed. A shrill laugh pealed out from below. I tucked my hand under my arm with the bow and slid sideways on my kernitian. Everyone around me spun in circles. Arrows whizzed past my face.

"Joshua!" Bo Chez turned his kernitian toward me, his eyes and mouth wide open in a mask of fear.

I slipped further. My good hand clutched my kernitian's mane. *So soft.* It slid through my grip.

"Hang on!" Charlie and Sam yelled. Leandro's cloak billowed across my face along with the scent of earth and chocolate.

I fell.

Someone grabbed me.

And then the world disappeared.

Chapter Thirty-One

Wind cut cool across my face, but the rest of me was warm. Leandro held me to his chest, urging his kernitian on, his heart pumping fast against mine.

My hand throbbed, wrapped in a rag, and Leandro's hair fell around me like a tent.

"Hekate struck you," Leandro said. "I still had some of the Moria plant in my bag and put the last of it on your hand."

"You caught me." It came out a whisper, but Leandro heard me and nodded.

Down below, Hekate and her army still raced along. They were dark shadows in the fog, stealing in and out of the mist. Arrows shot up toward us but fell short. We were too high for them to reach us now. Then they disappeared, and we flew for a long while as lavender light spread out soft on the horizon toward The Great Beyond.

"There." Bo Chez pointed to an opening ahead with a grim face. "I'm setting down in that field."

"But we're safe up here," I said.

"I'll hold them off with my storm power while you all fly to the power mill and find Finn."

"No! We *all* keep flying and get Finn."

"Do what I say, Joshua!" He flashed me a look that told me I'd better obey.

A trumpet rang out, strong and forceful. "Wait, do you hear that?" I said.

Behind me, the fog parted and our enemy was outlined clearly, rushing toward us again. The army drew closer with Hekate still in the lead. She kicked her horse on even faster. Flames streaked out of the cadmean beasts' mouths as they raced along. The Child Collector leaned over his horse, whipping him, and the vapes spat out their deadly tongues.

"Bo Chez, I came here to get Finn and that's what we're doing—together! We can't get separated again." I strained to see the power mill on the horizon and gripped my kernitian's fur tighter.

"I will find you," Bo Chez said.

"No!"

"Look." He pointed down at Hekate. "There's no time! Do you want to get us all killed?"

"I survived so far without you telling me what to do. Trust me, Bo Chez. Please!"

He shook his head, his jaw pulsed in a hard line. "You're just a boy!"

"I'm *not* just a boy, and what about you? Trust

you? You lied to me my whole life about everything!"

"I had to protect you."

"I know I'm not your grandson, but stay with me." I was pleading now, terrified of never seeing him again.

"You *are* my grandson."

"No. I'm not."

"In my heart you are."

"If I was, then you wouldn't be leaving me now!" All my suffering exploded through me. "I don't belong on Earth. I don't belong here. And I don't belong with you!"

"Enough!" Bo Chez's voice shook like thunder, his eyebrows jagged points.

In a small voice, Charlie said, "Joshua, let's just do what he says."

But it made me madder and madder that Bo Chez wanted to leave me. It hurt bad. "Your lightning orb probably led the Child Collector to our house. He could have gone somewhere else. Stolen some other kids!"

Leandro crushed his hand into my shoulder and I winced. "Joshua, if you didn't have the orb you would be dead. The Child Collector could have taken your friend by chance like hundreds of kids are taken every year."

Sam and Charlie remained curiously silent.

"There's no time for this, Joshua," Bo Chez said, dismissing me as he turned to zoom down. "Hurry, all of you!"

There was no holding back my growing anger or my hurtful words. This place and its myths had taken everything from me. My world. My home. My mother. My best friend. My grandfather. Even my sense of who I was.

"You let my mother die." I said it quietly, but he heard me.

Bo Chez's face crumpled. He opened his mouth to say something, but Leandro cut him off. "We'll all go down. You trap them first, sir, and we'll help fight until you contain them. Then the rest of us will get Finn." There was no time to respond. Leandro directed the kernitians, and we charged down as I wished this all to be over.

Wished I could disappear.

Wished I wouldn't die with those last awful words to Bo Chez on my tongue.

Bo Chez landed first and jumped off his kernitian into the open field. His thick arms swung through the air. Hail as big as baseballs crashed down on Hekate and her army. Horses buckled to the ground. Cadmean beasts howled. Soldiers screamed as their mounts crushed them. But still they kept coming.

The rest of us landed in the field behind Bo Chez. He was a madman. His pointed hair glinted like steel knives in the mist. Leandro threw me arrows then turned, threaded an arrow to his bow, and fired again and again. My fingers ached and shook as I pulled back my bow.

We fired arrows upon our enemies, and the cries of pierced soldiers filled the air.

And still, they drew closer.

I ran out of arrows and gripped the lightning orb, ready to throw it. *But where to aim it?* The Child Collector came into view, and I flung the orb. It skimmed the good side of his face and exploded on the ground past him. He screamed and fell off his horse. Hekate raised her hand. Blue sparked from her fingertips.

Bo Chez stomped the ground with one foot and swept his arms up. Wind blew up in a funnel before us, like a glass tube, surrounding Hekate and her men and separating them from us. They tried to break through the clear tornado but couldn't. Hekate's horse bucked, pawing at the walls of the storm funnel to break through. Her army had no better luck. They were trapped in the eye of the storm.

Bo Chez shook his hands in the air. Rain fell inside the storm circle. Terror filled me at what Bo Chez had unleashed. He didn't need the lightning orb for power. It was all inside him. Telling stories at home, he'd gesture with his big hands—and now he was acting out those stories.

And so was I.

The orb sailed through the tornado, cutting through the wind. It moved toward me and fell into my hand, warm from battle.

"Get Finn!" Bo Chez's voice came to us on the winds he ruled. "I'll hold them off."

Leandro pushed Sam, Charlie, and I toward the four kernitians who had bravely waited for us, and again we rode off into the sky. As we rose, Bo Chez grew smaller and smaller, no longer a titan.

Leandro coaxed us on. "Faster! To the power mill. Let's hope Finn was taken there!"

Charlie hollered a French war cry as we raced along. He gripped his kernitian's neck, his long legs folded up so far his knees touched his ears. Sam's wizened face crinkled in a smile and Leandro spurred his stag on, a fierce warrior.

And in that moment, as we came together for the same cause, I knew for sure we could fight our way out of this together, and all of us missing kids could benefit from the fight. A rush of words spilled out as my plan formed. Leandro, Sam, and Charlie nodded— they were in.

Behind me, Bo Chez was gone from view, and soon lights pierced the gloom ahead. We had reached the power mill.

For the last time.

Chapter Thirty-Two

We landed before the power mill. Its scattered broken windows and sagging roof didn't intimidate me now. It sat, sad and pathetic, like a homeless person on a bench in the park. *Chooga-chooga* boomed through the air and tugged on my nerves. The lightning orb pulsed a soft blue between my fingers, beating in sync with my own thumping heart. Leandro aimed his bow at the giant double doors to the power mill.

"Blast it good, Joshua, so we can go home," Charlie whispered.

The words over the door caught my eye again: *Bring light of life upon this land, for death awaits you in the resting. Toil on!*

"Yeah, well, death awaits you now," I muttered. "How about that, Lost Realm?"

I threw the orb at the door. It exploded, and I

staggered back as wood nicked my arms and face. Only a jagged hole with flamed edges remained of the door, and the *chooga-chooga* died as wheels creaked to a stop. Boys stared at us from inside the power mill.

Four guards slowly rose from where they'd been knocked to the floor. Leandro pulled back his bow. One. Two. Three. Four times. The guards collapsed—and this time, they didn't get up. The lights around the power mill dimmed and smoke chugged slower from its chimney, belching a final spew before disappearing.

All four of us stepped through the shattered doors and over the guards. Their vape spears lay on the floor, hissing. Sam picked them up. He handed us each one. It vibrated in my hand with a hot tingle.

"Point the vape away from you," Sam said. "Whoever holds a vape commands its powers. Just point it at your target and press this button on top."

My vape's tongue flicked in and out. I now commanded the power that had destroyed my mother—and I wanted the chance to use it.

Dozens of eyes fixed on us. None of them Finn's.

"Are there any other guards here?" Leandro said loudly.

Sweat broke out across my face from the steamy heat inside the power mill. No one spoke for a long moment. Then a skinny boy stepped forward. "Only these four. The others left with Hekate and the Child Collector."

From the silence burst questions. "Where'd you come from?" "Are we saved?" "Can we go home?"

I held up the vape, its power demanding silence, and the cries faded away. Hundreds of boys stared at me with desperate eyes, their breaths pumping in and out eager for rest and rescue. "You're all going home. But we haven't got time."

I quickly told them our plan to fly them all to the Lightning Gate on kernitians and send them home through the Lightning Road. "Let's go."

Cheers rose up through the power mill as kids scrambled down to us. Their sour, hot wind rushed over me. There was Lo Chez! He grinned as he ran past. The curse had ended. And through the craziness, a familiar voice called my name.

"Joshua!"

Finn! Through the grates, he poked his head out from the third floor. He waved to me with both hands. He was the best thing I'd seen in a long, long time. His smiling face shut this world out: the evil Hekate, the disgusting Child Collector, the red-eyed beasts, the sweaty power mill, death in The Great Beyond.

I pushed against the impatient kids going down as a garble of accents raced around me. All I'd been through was for this moment. This place wouldn't get to keep us. Then Finn was in front of me.

He punched me twice on the arm. "Ham." That kind of hurt felt good.

"And cheese." I punched him back.

Other kids hollered at us as they passed, but it was like me and Finn were the only ones there. He grinned so wide his eyes disappeared into tiny slits and his freckles looked like they'd pop. We started talking at once.

"Finn, I thought you were—"

"You came to rescue me?"

"And Bo Chez! He's from this world too. I was so scared—"

"Bo Chez? No way!"

"—you were dead." I finished up.

"You saved me, Joshua."

We punched each other at the same time and laughed, then ran down the steps of the power mill.

Finn pointed to my weapon. "Nice spear."

"Nice outfit." I yanked on his purple shirt.

He laughed then grew serious. "Sorry I didn't recognize you in the castle. I just couldn't believe you were there. For me!"

"It's why I came."

We grinned at each other. "Ready to catch a ride out of here?" I said.

He just nodded. "Come on!"

With a signal from Leandro we walked outside. He had released the other kids from the nearby bunkhouse, and they added to the crowd. I looked up into the gray sky. Earth was out there somewhere, far from Nostos, and we were helping change life for both.

I put an arm around my best friend to introduce him. "Finn." Sam and Charlie smiled, and Leandro gave me a big nod. Then I called out to my animal friends. Leandro joined me. Together we asked the kernitians to help us once more. Finn stared at me, amazed, but there was no time to explain. Would they come? They certainly didn't owe us a thing.

Then again, even animals, at times, like to play the hero.

Through the murky haze the kernitians came. The first few landed before us and they kept coming. Enough to carry every last one of us to the Lightning Gate. It was Sam who would take them there.

We showed the scared kids how to mount the flying deer. One boy cried.

"It'll be okay," I told him, and helped him up.

When all the kids were loaded, I nudged Finn. It was time to say goodbye again, but this time by choice. "Go with Sam. Get through the Lightning Gate and get home, okay?"

Finn turned to me with wild eyes and pink cheeks. "No way, Joshua. After all this? We stick together."

"Ham?"

"And cheese."

My legs felt like jelly as they let go of all the tension I'd been carrying in them, and I leaned my head on his shoulder, then pulled away. "Cool," was all I could say. We both blew out big breaths at the same time then laughed, the awkward moment gone.

The power mill lights flickered and the smoke from its work slipped away. The bulbs atop the power poles exploded like a string of Christmas lights popping one by one. The light inside the power mill surged, then dimmed again.

Leandro told the kernitians where to go and pulled the Lightning Gate key from his satchel. He hesitated for a moment, then handed it to Sam. "You've suffered greatly from the curse," he said. "I hope your trip to Earth brings you new life."

Sam nodded solemnly and tucked the flattened box into the top of his pants. He would send this first group through the Lightning Gate while the rest of us rescued the others from the remaining workhouses. He only needed one other thing.

"Here's the codes." I handed him the bottle. "And here, take my vape. You may need an extra."

And I thought of Bo Chez holding off Hekate and her army. What if something happened to him? Could I go home if Bo Chez didn't survive? The idea seized me like a Child Collector and wouldn't let go.

"Bo Chez," was all I managed to say.

"He'll be all right, Joshua," Sam said through his wrinkles, cocking his head. "He knows you didn't mean what you said."

But there was no way of knowing. "Light of Sol go with you, Sam."

"You too." He motioned for the kids to follow him as he rose in the air. His vapes pointed the way. I had to believe I would see him again.

Then Leandro, Charlie, Finn and I took off for the bakehouse, leaving the darkened power mill behind us.

Chapter Thirty-Three

The smells that greeted us as we neared the bakehouse made my stomach rumble, remembering that tasty agrius beast.

Finn clung to his kernitian and peered anxiously below.

"You won't fall off, I promise," I said.

He just shook his head and clung tighter. "Scary."

"Not as scary as being picked up by those monster birds."

"Jeez, did they stink!" Finn said.

"And not as scary as riding that Lightning Road," I said.

"Yeah, with that smelly Child Collector."

"He's nasty, isn't he?"

"Would I ever like to whizzle on him," Charlie said with a disgusted groan, and explained to Finn about the mizzle-whizzle thing.

Finn snorted. "Yeah, mizzle is definitely *not* enough for that creep. We could rain a triple whizzle-fest on him."

We all laughed together as if we were doing something normal, like hanging out at a baseball game, or biking, or building a fort, not flying on magical creatures through a strange land.

The moment over, we landed on the forest floor. The outline of the bakehouse blended into the trees. No light shone through its windows with the power out across the Lost Realm.

We found ourselves at a small back door. There was no sound of any baking going on: no machines mixing, no chefs yelling, no pots banging about. Smoke slunk from the chimney above in a pitiful spew. I pulled down slow on the heavy metal latch, but it wouldn't budge. A chill moved through me.

"We have to blast our way in again," I whispered, and pulled the orb out of my pocket, motioning for my friends to get back.

Finn said, "Hey, isn't that—" I flung the orb at the door.

White light blazed before us and made smithereens of the door. The orb floated back and fell into my hand, its electric power surging through me. Finn's mouth hung open. Once again, there was no time to explain.

The detonation blew out a hole larger than the door itself. Tiny fires spit around the edges, the smell of burnt wood sizzling in the air. Leandro stepped into the darkness, his vape and dagger ready. Charlie held tight to his vape while Finn clutched the back of my shirt.

I followed Leandro into the black hole and bumped into him as soon as we entered the room, then saw why. The only light in the room was a small candle burning on a table, and around it were four guards, the card game they were no longer playing spread out before them. They pointed their vapes at us.

One of the guards jabbed his vape in the air. "What have we here?"

Leandro was calm. "Just a group who means you no harm if you release the children."

The guard grunted. "Are you the reason we lost power?"

"Yeah, and you'll lose a lot more than that if you don't let us in," I said, getting madder by the second and running out of patience with this world. "Where are the kids who work here?"

"We locked the Reekers in the main hall." The guard flicked his finger to a door behind him. "But it won't matter to you because you're not getting in there."

The men moved around the table to face us, their four vapes to Leandro's and Charlie's two. The lingering scent of cooked meat now stunk.

Leandro smiled at the men, lowered his vape, and put his dagger away. "We don't want any trouble, just the children. Hekate has taken over the Lost Realm, and it doesn't look like Zeus cares to interfere with her plans."

The one guard stepped closer, his stink wrapping around me like a cloak. "And we're to guard the children until she returns. We should lock you in the basement, and then Hekate can decide what to do with you. I'm guessing it won't be fun."

Leandro smiled at him. "Hekate won't be coming back."

The guard frowned, his voice a low growl. "And why is that?"

Charlie's vape hissed at its competition across the room.

Leandro just kept smiling. "She's been delayed in a storm."

"What storm could—"

Before he could finish, Charlie's arm shot up. *Zap. Zap. Zap.* Three guards disappeared in a blaze. The last guard jerked away, but Leandro zapped him and he vanished in a streak of light. A fried onion stench floated over me and was gone.

Charlie stood taller. His vape's tongue flickered with a satisfactory hiss. "It's not our day to die."

"Wow." Finn's mouth hung open again.

"Yeah, wow, Charlie," I said.

He flicked his bangs away and hunched over again then Leandro gathered his cloak and together we kicked at the door to the main hall until it crashed down. The force ricocheted up my leg, fueling on my adrenalin to finish this mission. A group of girls and boys stood before us. Gloomy light stretched across the tops of their heads from windows covered in crooked metal bars, casting dull-striped silhouettes on the floor.

"It's over," I said, stepping out of the shadows. "Time to go home."

Red, the girl from the auction pit, came toward me. "Are the guards gone?"

I nodded. "We vaporized them, but now we've got to make it to the Lightning Gate—and fast—to get you home." The kids were silent, as if they didn't believe me. Some peered behind us as if expecting to see the guards.

"It's true." Leandro held up his vape and shook it. It hissed to the crowd before us. Some took a step back, but not Red.

"The guards have been whispering about some Oracle come to take over their world. Someone with powers." Red walked toward Leandro. "Is that you?"

"I fear it is not." Leandro looked at me.

Red figured it out and turned to me. "But I hear Hekate wants you dead. Why? Because of your powers?"

I shook my head, not having words to explain, but Red persisted. "Show us your powers."

The kids began chanting her words, ringing in my ears like the chants of the korax.

"Powers! Powers! Show us your powers!"

They stomped their feet, the call grew deafening, and the pounding words pumped through me faster and faster, my new destiny shaping inside me. I had the power to help not just one but many.

"Enough! Stop!" I held up my hands and the kids instantly fell silent, driving a new feeling of power within me. They were listening to me, trusting me. "If you want to get back to Earth, we have to go now."

"He's right," Red said. "Let's go."

I nodded at her, grateful, and Charlie and Finn led the quieted kids outside while Leandro grabbed what food he could and I called more kernitians for help. It was really happening—we'd soon be leaving Nostos and its Lost Realm.

Leandro placed his hand on my shoulder and its strength vibrated into me.

Stolen kids filled the clearing behind the bakehouse and Charlie and Finn helped them mount the kernitians. Charlie chose to lead this group to the Lightning Gate and return to meet us at the greenhouse. He sure didn't need to follow me anymore.

"Charlie?" I said. "Watch out for getting mizzled on."

"Or whizzled!"

"I told you mizzle was a real word," Red yelled down to me.

Charlie then charged into the air, his vape pointed like a lance. The kids followed him as if he were their hero leading their rescue.

And I guess he was.

Chapter Thirty-Four

We landed at the greenhouse. Torch flame licked across the glass building, illuminating it like sun splashing through a crystal. It felt good to pick rocks and smash the words etched in glass over the main door: *Mortal seeds cast into the soil of life feeds those worthy of its rewards. Reap on!*

I smashed the glass harder. *Reap this, you stinkers!*

Leandro quickly vaporized two surprised guards and released the kids we found in the cellar. They were dazed and covered in dirt but smiles lit up their faces when we explained the plan. Then we called the kernitians back and they arrived with Charlie in front.

"The kids are going through the gate," Charlie yelled as he landed.

"By the gods, the Earth code does work," Leandro said.

"Do you think Bo Chez is still holding off Hekate?" I said.

"If he can, he will," Leandro reassured me.

We loaded up the kids, and Finn wanted to help Charlie get them back to the Lightning Gate.

"Are you sure?" I tugged on Finn's shirt. He did look ridiculous in his purple outfit.

"Totally!" He punched me twice on the arm and I punched him back, but neither of us smiled this time. An urgency rattled my insides. It felt like time—and our luck—was running out.

"But my whole point in coming here was to get you back home," I said.

"We both will. Here's to our greatest adventure, just like your grandfather's stories."

"Yeah."

We punched each other's arm at the same time, but our punches fell soft, and his terrified face from my attic flashed through my head along with my own fear of watching him be sucked away. We stood there for a moment, not saying anything. What else was there to say?

We shared a bong bong from Leandro's supply and a long drink then Finn boarded his kernitian, and the group lifted off in a blur of hooves. My best friend, the one I came here to rescue, disappeared again but this time I carried hope of seeing him soon. Then Leandro and I flew alone on the way to our final stop: the castle.

The crumbling spires poked up from the treetops as the fog sucked at it. We landed to find that no soldiers guarded the castle. Its stone walls held no terror for me now. The giant doors stood slightly open, an invitation to enter, and we stepped into the dark hallway. Wall torches pathetically spit smoke and flames as we crept down the shadowy passage to the king's throne room.

Flickering light stretched from the open doors to the Great Hall. Leandro peered in and pulled the heavy door open with a screech. The chandeliers that once burnt bright were dark. Dim light came from torches that gasped out curls of smoke. Darkness stretched long across the massive room and in it the shadows moved, coming for us. I grabbed Leandro's arm, ready to run, but it was only the torch flames casting their figures on the walls. He pointed to the end of the Great Hall, and there sat King Apollo on his cracked and charred royal pavilion, chin down. Chains wrapped around his body and throne and were padlocked to one of the pavilion's legs. The once blazing logs in the fireplace now glowed a dying red. We headed for him, but he didn't even look up.

Leandro stopped at the foot of the pavilion. "King Apollo, where are all your guards?" He put his dagger away but pointed his vape at the king. It hissed, ready to strike.

The king slowly looked up. "Gone." He put his chin back down.

"Gone where?"

"To that traitor. I suspected Hekate's mission for a while, but not even Zeus would spare me a few Storm Masters to fight her. He had other places to protect he deemed more worthy."

"Where are the children?" Leandro thrust the vape in the air, inches from the king.

"The children?" King Apollo looked at Leandro in confusion.

"Yes, your servants: the Reekers, ignorant Barbaros. Where are they?"

The king's head lolled to one side. "I had a son long ago. But he never got the chance to grow up." He turned to me with a sad face.

"But your son, Sam, is here now and sick. He could die," I blurted out. "You've got to help him."

"Ah, that one deserted me." The king shifted in his chair, pushing against his chains.

"Like you deserted your own people?" I shot back.

His arms curled in to fold on his stomach. He wouldn't answer.

"If you help us fight off Hekate and her army, you can get your kingdom back, Your Majesty," Leandro said. "You must have some guards loyal enough to turn on her, but you'll need to stop stealing mortal children for power and find another way to light your land."

"It's impossible." The king seemed to sink deeper into his chair. He was so pathetic, how could he have ever ruled a whole land? Sam was more kingly than his own father. "I put Hekate in charge of the mill to satisfy her need for power. But she's greedy. She wants more."

"She wants it all," Leandro said. "She's evil immortal magic. She most likely has had a spell over you, my Lord. We must stop her."

"The other lands might help you this time," I offered.

The king sighed. "I wasn't ruthless enough to stop Hekate. And I wasn't always like this, you know. Do you believe me?" He leaned forward. I had no answer, and he slumped back down. "I used to be handsome and thin with fire in my belly. I once cared about my people, but Hekate changed things, changed me. Who would help me now?"

"We would," I said, not knowing how but eager to stop the witch.

Leandro put his hand on my shoulder. "The boy is right." His forceful voice caused the king to twitch up, wide-eyed. "I'm Leandro of the Arrow Realm and once a work camp guard, but now a fugitive as I seek my lost family. And I have supporters across Nostos who could help."

His last words echoed around the hall. The king glanced at his chariot that sat tossed to the side, broken and sad. "My people were great once. Could be again, but we fell away."

"Now is the time to stand on your own," Leandro said.

"If we only had special powers … ."

"You don't need powers to do the right thing," I said, this fact dawning on me as I spoke the words.

The king sat up straighter, cleared his throat, and said in a commanding voice. "As king I can pardon you, Leandro of the Arrow Realm. And a king's pardon extends throughout all realms."

"Only if you remain king." Leandro lowered his vape and his voice. "Come with us."

The king looked from me to Leandro and back again, and in his face I saw a glimpse of Sam and the young man he might have once been.

"Someone recently taught me that sometimes you must trust on faith." Leandro gave me a small smile. "Even if you must befriend an enemy to battle a greater evil."

Good thing I'd been right about him.

"First we have to stop Hekate and her soldiers," I said.

"Agreed," Leandro said. "If she takes over the Lost Realm, she'll move on to conquering other realms. Even if you get home again, Joshua, you won't be safe. And you, King Apollo, will be eliminated. Are you ready to die yet?"

He thought about it, then shook his head. "Not yet." He grasped the arms of his chair, strength coming back to him. "Hekate locked the children in the dungeon and took the key." He pointed at a wall sconce. "But I have another set hidden there. It's a master key and will unlock my chains."

Leandro strode to the sconce, reached in deep, and pulled out a large set of keys. They clanged as he unlocked King Apollo.

The king then stood, his head no higher than Leandro's chin, and tugged down on his purple vest.

Leandro bowed. "Lead the way, sire."

Apollo strode out of the Great Hall. Leandro explained our plan to him as we made our way to the dungeon. The king sure moved fast for a man who was just feeling sorry for himself.

Now he had purpose. So did I.

Chapter Thirty-Five

Leandro, the king, and the kids we set free from the dungeon all stood with me outside the castle. But this was no happy fairytale. It was grim and gory and real.

And there was still a job to do. We called and called, but this time no gold-antlered beasts floated down from the darkening sky. I glanced from treetop to treetop that faded in and out of the mist. *Come on!* I would not spend a fourth night on Nostos. Could not.

Leandro frowned. "Something's wrong. They should have returned by now."

The growing murmur of the kids jangled inside me as we waited, hope disappearing, and the fog slithered around my feet, chaining me to this place.

Then an awful thought struck me. "What if Hekate's army escaped Bo Chez's storm?" And the words I couldn't say sucked my breath up. *What if Bo*

Chez was dead?

"That could have spooked the kernitians enough to retreat home," Leandro said, searching the sky. A weariness settled over him and his face filled with something I hadn't seen there before—fear.

King Apollo looked up at the silent trees reaching down for us with their broken fingers. "We may not survive this."

"We know," Leandro said flatly. Fear snuck back— of total failure, of never seeing Finn or Bo Chez again ... of death.

The protests of the kids grew louder, wanting to know when they were going home. "For the love of Olympus, let me think!" Leandro held up his hands, and silence fell.

An idea came to me and, wild and gross as it was, it just might work. "What about the korax?"

Leandro turned to me. "What about them?"

"They fly."

Charlie's eyes bulged and he shook his head fast, biting his lip.

"You expect their help?" Sam looked to the sky and back at me. "They serve Hekate and are unpredictable, like the kernitians."

Leandro looked doubtful too. "I don't know, Joshua. I've seen good men die by their talons."

"Good men that they were forced to kill?"

"Yes."

"Sam, maybe the kernitians are unpredictable, but sometimes they come to help. Maybe the korax would help too." I spread my hands out with the thought.

"*Oui*, but the kernitians are like Santa's reindeer not birds from a scary monster movie," Charlie said.

"Would you rather call the cadmean beasts?" I snapped at him, tired of arguing about it.

Charlie flinched, and I felt bad for yelling at him, but then he slowly nodded and struck the air with a finger. "*D'accord!* Korax it is!"

"Hekate does treat them badly and keeps them in poor conditions, separated from their families," Sam said.

Leandro added to that. "Maybe if they believe they can be free of her torment and control, they may help us."

"And maybe they'd like to be heroes too," I said.

Leandro nodded. "And maybe they'll listen to the king."

We all looked at King Apollo, who studied the sky. "I will do my best to appeal to them."

Disgust filled me at the thought of riding the backs of those beasty birds—but we were out of options. We appealed to the great korax that once clapped Earth children in their talons and carried them away. Then Leandro put his hand on my arm and pointed to the sky. It darkened with a heavy black cloud. They were coming and fast. The kids behind me cried out, but I yelled at them to trust us, it would be all right. If not, we'd be all be dead.

Their canopy wings soared between the trees, then they pulled them in to their sides and glided down before us. Dozens of them. Black as the night with electric green eyes. Their enormous beaks clamped shut and they stood before us in silent rows, as if awaiting orders. One stepped forward and bowed its head. "Light bringers," it croaked. "Why dare call us?"

"You're our only hope and we can be yours." I talked to them, then motioned for the king to say something.

The king hesitated then finally spoke. "I promise you a better life, one free of Hekate. Now, please, take us to the Lightning Gate."

The leader hobbled forward, green eyes gleaming at us. Its claws, with curved knifepoints, could shred me in an instant.

"Oracle?" The question hissed on the breeze.

"No," I said.

"Light bringer?"

I hesitated for just a second before answering. "Yes."

The monstrous bird spread its wings and bowed its head with a cackle. "We serve."

I climbed on board with Leandro behind me, trying to ignore the bird's rotten smell. It was hard to grasp the slippery feathers of the korax, but it was better than being clamped in talons. "Find a partner and ride together," I told the kids waiting on the ground. "Hold on tight."

King Apollo was the first to move. He swung himself up on a bird. He got comfortable, then called to the kids. "Come now, you want to go home, don't you?"

The kids moved forward. When everyone had boarded a bird, we took off. Far in the distance, The Great Beyond beckoned with its soft purple. Had those Takers who'd attacked us finally stopped screaming and just floated along now waiting to die?

I wouldn't surrender like that. Leandro gave me a nod as he clutched the korax with one hand, the other wrapped tight around his vape. His strength—and the strength he'd helped me see in myself—made me want to fight whatever was ahead.

I threw my fist in the air and—like Charlie—gave a great warrior's cry.

Chapter Thirty-Six

We sped toward the Lightning Gate with victory in our heads as we crossed over the village of the Lost Realm. For the first time, figures emerged from the houses to watch us fly over. Some pointed at us.

The clearing appeared—Bo Chez still held off Hekate's army, but the tornado funnel flickered as if losing power. Hekate reared up on her horse, leading the charge to escape this magical storm weapon. Bursts of blue light exploded, and she broke through the wind funnel. It closed behind her, leaving her army trapped, and she headed for Bo Chez.

Lightning bolts burst from Bo Chez's hand, splitting the mist like a whip to water, but Hekate's fingers zapped her blue bullets back as she shot across the meadow. Bo Chez dodged left and right. And then a streak of light struck his hand. He cried out with a great roar of defeat—and the effort of holding back

Hekate became too much. He staggered and fell.

"Bo Chez!" I couldn't stand to watch as we flew closer, but couldn't tear my eyes away. "No!"

I commanded the other korax to take the kids and the king to the Lightning Gate. They flew off, and Leandro and I zoomed down. His grip tightened on me as we fell from the sky like an arrow released from his bow. The wind rushed by so fast my eyes teared up and everything became a blur. The meadow floor loomed, and we soared across it toward the fight, trees whirling past us. Bo Chez stumbled up and slashed his lightning bolts at Hekate. She twisted and turned away from them in a battle dance, her back to us. Bo Chez stumbled again.

I held the orb tight in my hand, ready to throw it, but was afraid of hitting Bo Chez. Hekate's horse bucked. Its hoof caught Bo Chez across the shoulder. He cried out and nearly fell. Hekate urged her horse on as if to trample him. He spun away just in time stretching his hands out to hold off his enemies, but they shook, then fell to his side.

And just like that the storm funnel vanished. Bo Chez could hold it no longer.

After a moment of confused silence the freed soldiers surged behind Hekate in a wave. She turned and saw us, gathered her reins, and bolted for us with her army, her vape fingers firing fast.

"Down!" I yelled, and Leandro shoved me into the bird's back as we flew over the witch toward Bo Chez and skimmed the ground. The end of the clearing rose fast. I commanded the bird to grab Bo Chez. Its talons snatched him up by his shirt, but then it swerved left to avoid Hekate's blasts, and in doing so Bo Chez slipped, hanging precariously from one giant claw.

"Bo Chez!" I reached for him, but Leandro was already bending down, straining to hold onto my grandfather's large frame. I lunged further over, nearly hanging upside down, and grasped Bo Chez's shirt. His face popped red as he tried to pull himself up. Fire streaked past me and our korax shrieked as blue flame struck it. The monster bird flapped its wings and Bo Chez was flung sideways, but he clenched feathers in his fists and held on tight as the woods advanced fast. Our crash was imminent when the bird turned right and circled the meadow. The wizard trees reached their arms out from the edge but couldn't stop us.

"Don't let go!" I felt Bo Chez slipping.

Bo Chez looked into my eyes like he had a hundred times, with frustration and humor and love. This look was none of those. This was regret.

"I'll always come for you," he said. His feet bounced on the ground as we jerked along. We were going down.

"Leandro, help!" The injured bird dipped and swayed with our efforts.

Leandro dared to look behind us. He still had one hand holding onto Bo Chez while he urged the bird on. "Hold on, sir!"

"Take care of my grandson."

"No!" Clutching at Bo Chez, I slid further off the

bird's back. Hekate's laughter filled my ears. So close.

And then hands gripped my leg, pulling me down.

Leandro couldn't save Bo Chez and me. His stricken face was the last I saw before falling onto Hekate's horse, slamming painfully into the saddle. She pulled me tight to her chest, and the sickening sweet stench of roses swarmed up my nose as I struggled to get free, but her magic hold was too strong. Trees flashed by in a blur.

She pointed to soldiers riding on her left. "Get to the gate and stop anyone from going through." They nodded in unison and veered away. I fingered the orb in my pocket, desperate but terrified to use it.

An agonizing cry pierced my ears, and I twisted my head around to see the great winged monster crash in the meadow, a flurry of feathers and dust. Bo Chez and Leandro spiraled through the air. They smashed into the trees and were gone.

"You," Hekate said to a soldier who rode near her, "go back. Find that Storm Master's lightning orb and bring it to me at the armory." The soldier bowed his head and swung around while we galloped along with the remaining army. I focused on the dead korax, hoping against hope that Bo Chez or Leandro would rise up from behind it.

Hekate twisted my head to the front. "Say goodbye to your friends. It's you and me, Oracle. And your fate is short lived."

Home was gone. My friends were gone. Bo Chez was gone. Nothing could keep me going now.

We slowed our pace and headed out of the field, into the woods. The soldiers fell into ranks behind us, two rows, side by side on our narrow path. The trees grew closer, creeping in on me like bars in a cage. Red eyes sprung from the murky woods and grew in number as black fur leapt at us from the fog. Cadmean beasts rode along now, and my cage grew smaller and more deadly.

The Child Collector trotted up beside us. "Taking him to the armory, Hekate?"

"Yes. I want a demonstration. Perhaps there's a use for him besides death."

"If not, let me at him." My stomach cramped and I squeezed my arms into my sides.

"We'll dispose of him together, brother," Hekate said.

That melted mess of a face leaned down into mine and I froze, staring at his one eyeball that flicked over me. "Reeker," he grunted and poked me with a stubby finger. "I should have taken that Storm Master down when I had the chance. Made him hurt for what he did to me."

"It's done," Hekate soothed, putting a pale hand on his filthy one. "Be glad he met his end."

I shuddered from the chilly mist and fear, as cold on the inside as I was on the outside. My cheek throbbed from where I'd smashed into the saddle, and every muscle in my arms screamed from pulling up on Bo Chez—yet I hadn't been able to save him.

Hooves clopped behind us in a battle rhythm, and

I looked at the ground, not wanting to stare into that eyeball for one more second, but the Child Collector leaned in closer and forced my head up, his rough fingers pressing deep into my chin. His stink replaced Hekate's roses, and the memory of losing my mother struck deep.

His eye twitched and his one good nostril flared with fury. "I would have become a solider to King Ares if it weren't for what your Storm Master friend did to me. I've only got one good eye now, but I'm watching you. And now that he's dead, you'll pay for his deed, Reeker." He massaged his face, as if reliving that night Bo Chez struck him.

I sunk deeper into the folds of Hekate's cloak, her evil preferable over his for the moment. She laughed and the Child Collector joined her. Their mockery stung like my face, and hope drained away of ever surviving the Lost Realm.

Chapter Thirty-Seven

Around a sharp bend, stone walls shot up before us. A round castle reared up and soldiers peered down from its turrets, bows in hand. The horses slowed to a walk, and we entered the armory below the forbidding message carved into its stone: *Vanquish all the weak and weary that pass. Only great souls may bear arms to conquer with might and strength. Ye gods!*

The cold inside me worsened with those words as we passed beneath the dank doorway. I brushed up against chipped stone and winced at its roughness. My thoughts were filled with two things: how to get away from Hekate and her men, and Bo Chez's last words: *I'll always come for you.*

Hekate dismounted, dragging me with her. I fell to my knees and cried out. I'd kept hope all this time we'd succeed, but now that was as broken as the blocks of stone that lined one side of the arena in jumbled piles, crumbled from the partially caved-in roof. The air floated thick with smoke from wall torches that coughed soot, and black wisps escaped into the gloom through the roof's hole. The soldiers entered on horseback behind us and lined the round arena. The cadmean beasts trotted in behind them and sat before their masters. All eyes were on me.

The Child Collector swung his large body off his horse and joined Hekate on a stone platform in the middle of the dirt pit. I stood, my legs shaking.

"You're not so powerful now without your Storm Master and his lightning orb, are you?" Hekate crossed her arms, assuming I'd borrowed the orb and given it back. Her robe hung torn and streaked with mud, her hair a gnarled mess from her encounter with Bo Chez. *Good*!

I shook my head and croaked out, "No."

"The orb is mine. Once we claim it from his body."

I flinched at the word 'body.' Bo Chez could never be a 'body,' or Leandro. They were larger than life. People like that didn't die—shouldn't die. My fear and sadness started to churn into something more, a crazy anger at all that had happened to me and the people I cared about.

"Perhaps we should shake the Reeker upside down, Kat, just in case he has it, to see if it falls out," the Child Collector said.

She held up her hand, then smoothed down her hair with it. "First, I want to see his powers."

"I don't have any—"

"Liar!" She motioned to the Child Collector. "Cronag, search his pockets."

He sneered and strode down the platform steps, coming at me. I stepped toward him and spit, wanting to make him mad. Everyone I cared about was gone. There was nothing to lose. He stopped in his tracks at my boldness, then came closer as the enemy crowded around me. A soldier urged his horse forward and more followed. The mist flowed around them, seeping between the cracks of the stone walls. In my exhaustion, faces seemed to float in the haze, like the ghosts of stolen children.

Step by step the soldiers inched toward me then stopped. Behind them weapons hung by hooks on jagged rock: bows, axes, pitchforks, swords. They clanked together from a small breeze and swung back and forth. My circle closed in. The Child Collector stood before me, his burned half-face a road map to hell while his vape flicked its killer tongue at me.

I came here because of Finn, but I wouldn't be leaving with him.

The Child Collector walked around me and jerked Sam's flute from my back pocket.

He inspected it. "It's made by the king's flute maker."

"Play it, Oracle," Hekate demanded.

The Child Collector thrust it into my hands, giving me no choice but to blow out a sad melody. The sheer butterflies floated down from treetops into the broken fortress. One landed on the Child Collector's shoulder. He picked it up with his stubby fingers, frowned at me, and then crushed it in his fist. The others disappeared back up into the fog.

Hekate flared her nostrils. "Very good, ignorant Barbaros. You carry the ancient musical talent of Apollo. Can you heal like him as well?"

"Even if I could, I wouldn't show you." I slid the flute into my back pocket, hoping the Child Collector would forget about my front pockets. He did, but gave me a punch to the head instead. The rock walls moved in and out then steadied themselves again.

Hekate crossed her arms and pointed to a trough on the side filled with water. "Make it move."

"The wood?"

"The water, you imbecile!" Hekate stamped her foot, her voice growing shriller. A sheen of sweat popped out on her forehead, and she wiped at it angrily.

"Forget it," I said, and dodged the Child Collector's fist just in time. He grabbed my neck and squeezed hard.

"Poseidon can. You can, Oracle." Her fingers clawed the air.

"I'm not your Oracle, witch." I didn't care what I said anymore. They were going to kill me anyway.

She glided toward me, as if her feet floated above the ground. A bruise highlighted her cheek. Where one of Bo Chez's hail balls had struck? *Good going, Bo Chez*. But with that, his death flooded through me all over again, and I squirmed to get loose, but the Child Collector's grip tightened.

Hiss. Hiss.

His vape threatened incineration.

"Move the water, or my brother will snap your neck," Hekate said. "And then the beasts can feast on you."

I dug at the sweaty hand that clutched me but couldn't break free, my neck burned. "I can't move water!"

"Teumesios!" She snapped her fingers. One of the cadmean beasts stood up. "Guard him."

The Child Collector let go, dropping me on my butt. The beast moved closer. It opened its mouth, panting at me with rotten breath that curled my insides. The soldier's horses pawed the ground, inching closer, and the weapons on the wall clanged like a battle alarm as they smashed about from a gust of wind.

This was not the ideal way to go. I scrambled back and stood up, palms out. "Stop!"

The beast did. "Why? You'd be a tasty meal," it said.

"Not tasty, and I'm not your dinner." The Child Collector shoved me toward the beast, but I shoved him back. His eyes widened in surprise, then he flung his vape in my face. The snake tongue flicked so close I felt the snap of its breeze on my cheek. My time was done. At least it would be over quick.

"Enough!" Hekate threw her hands up.

The Child Collector lowered his spitting vape.

"Soon, boy."

"Never, Cronag." I spit at him again.

The cadmean beast raced around us, barking and snarling, its thick tail whipping my arms. "Reeker meat! Reeker meat!"

"Back, Teumesios," Hekate ordered, and the beast trotted back to the wall. Then she pointed at me with a trembling finger. "You carry the power of Artemis too, malumpus-tongue."

That's when spoken words pulled me back from the edge of death. "That's because he comes from the Arrow Realm, like me."

"Halt," a soldier yelled. I turned around fast. Leandro sat on a horse in the doorway. He leaned to one side in his saddle as if in terrible pain, a gash across his forehead, and his cloak was covered in dirt. But he was the most awesome thing I'd ever seen.

A rush of soldiers rode by me on horseback toward him. They blocked my view, surrounding Leandro, their horses cutting up the ground around him.

"Back," Hekate commanded her men, and they parted the way. "Let me see him."

Leandro sat up straighter with a grimace and walked his horse slowly into the circle of Hekate's men. One of her soldiers lay unconscious across the saddle in front of him—and behind him he led Bo Chez on a rope.

Chapter Thirty-Eight

"**B**o Chez!" He staggered and went down on one knee, but Leandro pulled him up. I looked at Leandro, wanting answers, but his gaze passed over me as if he didn't even know me.

Leandro pushed the unconscious soldier off his horse and he hit the ground with a thud, but didn't move. "He's not dead, but he'll have one bad headache when he comes around. He took me by surprise, but didn't fare well."

A soldier dragged his moaning friend away.

"Remove his weapons," Hekate ordered. A soldier moved forward, but Leandro held up his hand and dismounted. He tugged Bo Chez along, my grandfather's big head hanging low, but I could still see the blood that trickled down the side of his head from a nasty cut and a red-purple bruise swelled on his cheek.

"I have none," Leandro said.

"We'll see about that," the Child Collector said, gripping my neck painfully again. I tried to wrench free but he squeezed tighter with his calloused hands. Struggling only rocketed more pain through me, so I forced myself to be still.

The soldier searched Leandro, finding nothing, then shoved him to his knees, taking Bo Chez down with him. I lunged forward but the Child Collector yanked me back and my teeth slammed together hard, vibrating into my jaw.

"I. Want. The. Lightning orb," Hekate said, emphasizing each word with icy calm.

"And I want to end this Storm Master for good," the Child Collector said. "Let me at him."

"Leave my grandfather alone!" Courage sparked in me at knowing Bo Chez was alive, but he shook his head at me.

Hekate turned to me, eyes wide like two black coals in her white face, and pinched her lips together in a red slash. "Grandfather? How lovely. Two family members with ancient powers. What luck."

The Child Collector shook me. "This filth is your grandfather?" He let one hand off me and twisted a grubby fist at Bo Chez, who tilted his head up just enough to look at the man he had scarred to save my life. "You dishonor the most honored post there is." He spat on the ground. "And your blast to my face killed any career as a soldier. I'd be out winning battles now, not collecting these Reekers, if it weren't for you.

You'll pay—and then some."

"Leandro, let him go," I said. "Why are you doing this?" He didn't answer me, his face set like stone.

"Yes, Leandro, let him go," Hekate said. "The Storm Master is mine."

Leandro looked around at the army before him, and Bo Chez hung his head again. The horses snorted and stomped the ground. The silence grew, as did the Child Collector's pressure on my neck. Through the roof's hole, tree branches bowed down as if listening—and waiting—and the soldiers collectively took a step forward on their horses, vapes ready to strike.

"I'll trade you the boy for the Storm Master," Leandro finally said, standing again and tugging Bo Chez up with him. "He would be most useful to you in battle."

"No!" I twisted to get free, but the Child Collector knocked me in the head. Pain flared, and the world became a shadowy shape for a second.

Hekate looked at Leandro. "And why would I trade the Reeker for him?"

"Because he's not the Oracle."

She stepped closer to him, her robe swirling angrily. "What do you know? Enough of this!" She waved her arms. "Soldier, search the Storm Master for his orb."

The man stuck his hands all over my grandfather but found nothing. The orb pressed against my leg, begging to be found, begging to be thrown.

"Where is it?" Hekate screamed, her wild eyes and hands scratching at the air inches from Bo Chez's face, her bruise a match to his. He flinched but didn't step back.

Leandro pointed at me. "He has it."

My heart sunk like an anchor inside me.

All heads turned to look at me. I wanted to disappear. The Child Collector kicked me toward Hekate, who now glared at me with narrowed black eyes like pits of poison.

All my loyalty and newfound love for Leandro dried up. I'd been angry enough to punch someone before but never wanted to kill them until now.

I wrenched the orb from my pocket before the Child Collector could stop me and threw it at Hekate. "Here!" The horse nearest her reared up, threw his soldier off, and in that instant a dozen vapes were aimed at me. Hekate's arm flew up and clamped the lightning weapon in her fist.

My one chance. Gone.

I got another bash to the head for that. Harder this time. Stars swam around me and I groaned with the blow. When my head cleared, Bo Chez watched me with a contorted face.

Hekate held the glowing orb in her pale hand and turned it over and over. Its blue faded. "Mine now. And so are you, Reeker. Until I'm done with you."

"He's not who you want, Hekate," Leandro said, who had calmly been standing by, still holding onto Bo Chez's rope. "He doesn't have all the ancient powers required to be the Oracle. He only has powers of two Olympians: Artemis and Apollo."

Hekate continued to stare at the orb, two red patches flaming her cheeks. "Go on."

"He may have blood in him from each land, and while it's rare that both would pass on their ancient power from the fallen gods to him, it's possible."

But my mother had been mortal. Bo Chez had said so. Or another lie?

Hekate turned back to Leandro and slid the orb into her robe pocket. "But his smell betrayed him."

"Perhaps your sense of smell is off. Perhaps you smelled him only because he holds powers of more than one Olympian, but not all—not enough to change our destiny and bring back the god's powers. And perhaps you've never encountered a Reeker like him."

Hekate paced before Leandro, a finger tracing her blood red lips. "Perhaps ... he couldn't command the water after all, supposedly. Tell me more."

Bo Chez just dangled there like a captured animal. *Show me what to do.* But he didn't. I was on my own.

"I work undercover for the Arrow Realm," Leandro went on. "I seek out those with the ancient powers to draft into work for Queen Artemis as soldiers or hunters."

He had said he didn't hunt kids on his land. Had he lied about that, too? I stared at him, remembering his knife pushed against my neck. A soft, cold rain began to fall through the hole in the roof and the wall below it glistened as raindrops pinged off the tree branches.

"I met up with this boy, who stole a lightning orb, and his friends, and this Storm Master"—Leandro jerked on Bo Chez's rope—"and thought it would be useful to stick with them for a while. I planned to lure them to the Arrow Realm under false pretenses. It would mean a big bonus for me to deliver mortal children to Queen Artemis along with a lightning orb and a Storm Master."

I didn't want to believe his words and yet it became clear. Leandro had betrayed us all.

"Explain what you were doing at Apollo's court." Hekate tapped her foot faster.

"I had taken the two boys as my captives and was informing King Apollo that I planned to take them to the Arrow Realm. It was a gesture of good will, being that I apprehended them in his land. Then the Storm Master showed up and changed my plan. And so did you." Leandro smiled then, and where it once so recently boosted my spirits, it now chilled my insides, for he'd revealed what he truly was. A thief, a liar, and a murderer.

"And where is the other boy?"

"He got sick so I eliminated him. Artemis wants strong, meaty slaves to feed the beasts, not sickly ones."

"Why should I trust you?" Hekate tapped her foot harder. The bruise on her cheek darkened, marking her like me.

Leandro's smile fell, and he pushed his hand into his side as if it pained him from where he crash-landed. I hope it hurt like crazy. "Come with me to the Arrow Realm and see for yourself."

Hekate exhaled deeply and glanced at her brother, who nodded, shaking me right along with him. "Perhaps Artemis and I can talk strategy, now that I've taken over the Lost Realm. It may help to have an ally." She swished a hand at me. "Take this one, for now. If I discover he's other than what you say, you'll pay with pain."

The Child Collector shoved me toward Leandro, who bowed at Hekate and then pulled me to his other side, holding me tight. I looked over at Bo Chez. Why didn't he do anything? What was wrong with him?

"And I'll take care of the Storm Master," the Child Collector said, curling his cloak in with his fists.

"First, we use him, then you can have him," Hekate said. "He'll be an asset in battle."

Bo Chez raised his head and finally spoke. "I'll never fight for you, Ancient Evil One." He straightened up, his Titanic body expanding the space it once hid in. In that instant he didn't look defeated at all. He looked angry and strong and full of power. "I'll defeat you again."

Hekate twirled in a circle around him. She stumbled and regained her balance, facing him, fingers frozen in the air. "Aha! You've aged, Storm Master. So this is the one who injured you, Cronag?"

"Yes." The Child Collector grunted, tugging his hat down lower over his face. Hekate glided to him and took his hand. She held it to her face, then pressed her other hand to his scarred cheek. He leaned his head in to hers, and for a moment only their deep synchronized breathing filled the quiet of the arena. I darted my eyes to Bo Chez for answers, but his eyes were focused on the two siblings. I pulled away from Leandro but choked as he ripped me back by the neck of my T-shirt. I kicked his leg, but he didn't move, just knotted my shirt tighter. I gasped for air and he loosened his hold enough to breathe while every muscle in me wanted to kill him.

Hekate broke the silence. "Then we shall have the pleasure of killing him, brother. And you shall have his body in place of the one he ruined."

A slow smile cracked along the good side of his face. "No better revenge than to use the very body that hurt me, and what a bonus to command his storm power as my own."

No! My stomach flopped and a sick taste swelled in my throat at the thought of the Child Collector possessing my grandfather's body. *Let me be dead before that happens.*

"Only for you, Cronag," Hekate said, and raised her hands.

Blue sparks crackled along her fingertips, poised to kill, and she cast her hands out. The horses twitched and the soldiers pulled at their reins as skittish hooves bit the arena floor. I lunged for Bo Chez, but Leandro held me back once again. I kicked his leg harder. He groaned this time but wouldn't let go.

Leandro yanked on Bo Chez's rope and his neck muscles bulged—then the rope snapped in two. Bo Chez swung his arms in the air and a storm cloud burst above him. Horses screeched. Leandro knocked me down and fell on me just as lightning streaked the air. We slammed into the ground, the breath knocked out of me.

"Bo Chez!" I rasped out. Leandro dragged me up and along the dirt, away from the firing zone, but Bo Chez stood his ground, a giant wielding his power. Hail and vape fire rained down.

Blast! Blast!

Bo Chez's body twisted as he was struck, again and again. He swayed but didn't fall. The cloud grew bigger. He swung his hands in an arc.

Hekate's pale hand thrust itself through the smoke. The orb pulsed blue in her fingers. I struggled to get out from under Leandro, but his hand pressed into me hard.

"Stay," he grunted in my ear.

Hekate drew her hand back.

"No!" I ripped into the dirt to pull myself out from under Leandro but couldn't break free.

Hekate let go. The orb rocketed toward Bo Chez. It sailed on blue vape fire, aimed to kill.

Boom! It raced around Bo Chez in a lightning lasso.

Light blazed. Smoke bit the air.

His storm cloud vanished, and Bo Chez fell to the ground.

He didn't get up.

Chapter Thirty-Nine

The smoke cleared. Bo Chez lay on his side. *Get up!* But he didn't. The orb sailed back to Hekate, and she plucked it from the air and slid it away.

"Take the body and place it in the ice cellar until we can use it later," Hekate ordered two soldiers. They nodded and dragged Bo Chez up.

"Bo Chez!" I began to sob and couldn't stop, falling to my knees as Leandro let me go. I crawled along the dirt pit, but a soldier kicked me to a stop. I lay there, gasping with tears and pain as the only family I knew was dragged off, his power and goodness hauled away like garbage.

Leandro picked me up and shoved the soldier who kicked me. "He's my property now. I don't want him damaged and costing me money, you brainless thug."

The soldier pulled out his knife, but Hekate shushed him. "Now, now. No fighting, boys."

The Child Collector strode to me and lifted my chin up as I hung in Leandro's arms. I had no choice but to stare into his one eye that crinkled with satisfaction. "Feel the pain. Own it. It's yours now, as mine was." He squeezed my chin hard, his scars flaring at me with rage. Dizziness overcame me, and the arena tilted. Then he thrust me back into Leandro. "Take this Reeker out of my sight, but watch out. He likes to bite."

Leandro gripped both my arms to my sides, and I let him hold me up as the Child Collector took his place next to his sister, putting an arm around her shoulder. This evil, unstoppable pair had taken away my everything.

"To the Lightning Gate and the Arrow Realm." And with Hekate's orders, Leandro pulled me to his horse and pushed me up on it.

"Let me go." I punched at him, but he forced me down in front of him. Hard leather slapped my cheek as I bounced off his saddle horn. There was no breaking away from his strength. Mine had left me. Bo Chez had left me—again. It was too much to hold inside. I looked behind us at Bo Chez's body being carted away by horse. He grew smaller and smaller as we left the armory, and tears stung my eyes, blurring the sight of the giant man who'd raised me, loved me … rescued me. I twisted my head back around, not wanting Leandro to see me cry. With each sob I breathed in bitter air, tangy leather, and Leandro's spice. I swallowed each breath with hate.

The rain slowed and stopped as we followed

Hekate and her men back down the wood's path, taking up the rear. Behind me, Bo Chez remained, his power silenced. I wanted to run back, shake his big shoulders, and tell him it was time to go home.

"You got him killed," I whispered as exhaustion filled my empty insides. Leandro didn't answer, but for a brief second his hand touched my shoulder. Then he snapped his reins to attention and dug his boots into the horse. Hooves beat into my head as the gray world of the Lost Realm threatened to lose me forever.

Leandro was a traitor.

My friends may not have made it out alive.

The lightning orb was gone.

Bo Chez was really dead.

My awful words to my grandfather stung my thoughts. *You let my mother die.*

I watched the ground fly by as we headed to the gate that would steal me away to yet another land. Then a silver speck caught my eye. It shone from the top of Leandro's boots. A hidden knife tucked inside.

And then Bo Chez's words came to me. *You must use the talents you were born with for all the good, no matter the cost.*

My friends might still need me. I couldn't abandon them.

I tried to lean down, but Leandro gripped me tighter.

"Just let me rest," I said. He hesitated, then freed me to lie on the back of the horse as we bounced up and down. Its wet mane chilled my cheek. My right arm hung down and my fingers grazed the top of Leandro's boot. We jerked left, avoiding a boulder in the path. Up we flew. Down we came, and in that second I gripped the knife's handle and pulled it out. It fit in my palm, tiny and deadly, and my only weapon now that the orb had a new owner. My heart thumped in rhythm with the horse hooves.

Two questions loomed. Who would I use it on, and could I?

We reached the meadow. I sat up, tightening my fist around the tiny dagger. Its sharp edge cut painfully into my palm.

Hekate's army galloped along single file. She led the way, her green robe soaring in and out of the fog like an evil magic carpet, and her brother rode just behind her, his fat body obscuring most of the view. Our horse leapt forward, its feet not seeming to touch the ground, and I held on to the saddle horn in terror as my hidden knife slit my skin. *Don't cry out!*

Then Hekate whipped her horse in a furious frenzy. "Get them! They can't get through!"

The Child Collector's horse turned left, freeing our view. A meadow opened up before us, and a tall structure unlike anything I'd ever seen before rose from the ground through the blowing mist. The army barreled toward it, leaving me and Leandro behind.

The Lightning Gate.

And at the foot of it, my friends were fighting for their lives.

The massive portal engulfed an area almost as wide

as the field and gleamed like a bronze coin, tarnished green in spots. It stood on round stone blocks, an awesome giant with the power to take me home. Its two standing columns were like the Greek Coliseum, and the column linked between them overhead appeared twice as thick around. Strange symbols and animals were etched in its metal like the ones from the cave: curly cues, scrolls, horned animals, monsters, figures with arms outstretched. They seemed to move along the columns as if trapped in a machine they couldn't leave, and the smell of scorched metal blew off the gate.

Across the top column in giant letters marched the words: *Honor the fire of Zeus that sparks your journey. Adversity breeds true power. Bow to the gods!*

This Lightning Gate had stood here for thousands of years, created from old magic. It held technology that didn't belong on this world. Its golden doorway pulsed with ancient power that had transported mortals and gods for centuries. It had stolen me away on a ribbon of cold fire and was the most amazing and beautiful thing I'd ever seen, but it didn't belong here. It belonged in a museum where it couldn't steal people.

Leandro rode off to the right, away from Hekate's army, and headed toward the woods.

I sat up straighter. "Where are you going?"

Light flashed at the gate, and it looked like the gate itself shot bolts of lightning. Soldiers on foot fired at a mass of kids under the giant structure. A tall boy blasted back with a vape. Charlie! And there stood King Apollo. And Sam herded the kids to safety behind the columns on either side. Could Finn be one of them?

We had come so far. Bo Chez was dead, but Hekate couldn't win. It wasn't fair.

I grabbed the reins, trying to lead the horse back to the battle but Leandro jerked them back. "My friends!"

"I'm trying to save them," Leandro said as he took us deeper into the woods.

"Where are you going?" I yelled. "Go back!"

Behind us the trees closed in, and the meadow and Lightning Gate vanished.

Leandro pulled us to a stop and leapt off the horse, holding onto the reins with one hand. Behind a boulder he lifted up his satchel and bow and arrows. He threw his satchel across his shoulder, swung his bow onto his back, and stuffed his arrows into his leg holder.

"You're a liar!" He would kill my friends and had to be stopped.

The horse snorted and jigged, and I tried to grab the reins again, punching the air at Leandro with his own knife, but he wouldn't let go. I kicked the horse hard. It shook its head and with a great roar sped off back to the meadow with me hanging on for my life. I had to finish this mission—even though the sorrow of losing Bo Chez weighed me down. Clutching the horse's mane, terror raced through my very veins as we streaked toward the gate. Leandro dragged along the ground beside me.

"Let go!" I kicked at him with my right foot, but he held on to the reins, shouting at me to stop.

We broke through the woods. I strained my eyes through the thickening mist to find Hekate's green robe. She had reached the Lightning Gate and raced back and forth, shooting with deadly fingers, her blue sparks flying against the glimmering bronze gate. In the midst of new events, it seemed she had forgotten about me and Leandro.

The Child Collector trotted off to the side, giving orders. The two dozen remaining soldiers formed a battlefront and, like a row of cannons, fired their vapes down the line. But the gate fired back. Arrows of light exploded from its metal, and soldiers fell, one by one.

Lather foamed at my horse's mouth, spattering on me as we raced toward the bloodshed. I focused on that green robe and headed for it. Leandro tried to hoist himself up on the horse, but I gave him another good kick and he fell back to the ground with a loud groan. Mud spit up from dragging him along.

"By the gods, boy, stop!" Leandro pleaded with me.

But I couldn't stop.

Closer. Closer.

Hekate's robe flew behind her, a flag I was determined to take down.

Leandro still clung to my horse as we raced toward the witch. Hekate toggled her head around, her mouth a surprised 'O' at seeing us. She yelled something to her men, bent over her horse, and cantered our way.

I faced her head on. Her fingers fired at me. I tugged my horse's reins to the left, then the right, the muscles in my arms screaming for relief. Leandro kept yelling at me to stop the horse, and then he was gone, rolling away behind me.

Closer. Closer.

She smiled at me, those blue teeth shining through malicious red lips and her bruise dark upon her face, marring her beauty that I'd so feared.

Hate drove me on.

I bashed into her, grabbed her robe, and we fell together.

Hooves threatened to trample me.

I slammed on top of her—a moment of doubt coursed through me—and shoved the knife deep within her flesh. She shrieked, her rose stench overpowering, and I pulled the dagger out. *No blood!* She grabbed my hand. Her icy fingers shocked me into loosening my hand on the dagger, and she tore it away, thrusting it in my face. "It will be fun to kill you like this, boy."

I knocked it out of her hands before she got the chance, and two arrows struck her shoulder. She fell backward, clutching at the arrows, and convulsed on the ground. With that opportunity, I scrambled through her robe pockets, ripping the gold-threaded quilt, and pulled out the lightning orb. Then her hand clenched my wrist.

"Let go!" As I struggled against her, my pencil poked into my leg. I ripped it out with my free hand

and stabbed her in the chest with all my force. *Draw that!*

She flopped on the ground, aiming a shaky finger at me. It crackled with blue sparks.

I jerked left, just missing her lightning bullets, and drew back the orb. "Your turn to die!"

But Leandro snatched me up onto his horse, swinging himself up behind me. He grabbed the reins of Hekate's horse, towing it behind us, and we flew toward the army that abandoned their fight at the Lightning Gate and now charged us.

I beat at Leandro with my fists, and headed toward my death.

Chapter Forty

"**G**et down." Leandro pushed me down hard onto the horse's back.

I finally gave in and held on tight. He drew back his bow and shot at the oncoming army. Arrows spun out in a blur. Men fell. Again and again.

"What are you doing?" I tried to sit up, but he shoved me down again.

"Trying to not get us killed."

What?

Before I could argue, he said, "Use the lightning orb!"

I couldn't argue with that.

We rocketed toward the soldiers, firing on them.

The roar of the fight pounded in my ears: the cries of men struck by the gate's power, the screams of horses slamming into the ground, the blasts of lightning exploding like fireworks in the smoldering air.

Charlie and Sam stood under the Lightning Gate, gunning their vapes at the two soldiers that remained behind. The cries of scared kids huddling behind the gate filled the air. King Apollo stood off to the side, his hands moving back and forth on a panel. Was he manning the Lightning Gate's guns? Then the gate unleashed more storm power. White light blasted from its bronze columns and struck the two soldiers. They fell off their horses and didn't get up.

A glance behind revealed Hekate shoving a soldier off his horse to hoist herself up on it. She slumped over the saddle horn, then joined her army and her brother. The enemy circled around us from the rear as we neared the gate. They were closing us in!

We galloped between the dead, their faces of agony stuck in their final moments. The scent of blood and mud and sweat rose from the fresh graveyard, and there was no escaping it. Hekate's horse ran fast beside us, leaping over bodies. Charlie and Sam jumped up and down under the gate, and the group of kids screamed. Finn's face popped up, then vanished behind the sea of kids.

Leandro whirled around and fired his bow. One. Two. Three. More soldiers disappeared behind us.

The Lightning Gate rose up fast. Leandro steered our horse left and we dashed alongside the massive metal sculpture. Sam grabbed Charlie and they ducked behind the gate as we passed it. Our eyes met briefly, and my heart clenched like a fist. My shoulders tightened and my lungs burned, ready to give up. *Not yet!*

Soldiers came at us, but their horses reared up when the gate fired at them, tossing the men in the air. Lightning cracked like a whip to their chests, and they crashed onto the ground. Only a few stumbled up. Leandro aimed his vape at them and they snatched up their vapes. Too late. *Zap. Zap. Zap.* They were gone, too. Their horses trotted about and then stood still, as if waiting for their owners.

The trees swayed in and out with deep angry breaths, and then a great creaking of wood screeched around us. Our horse bolted up in terror as giant tree limbs that had grown down and burrowed in the ground came to life and ripped themselves from the earth. They swung in the air like great elephant trunks and reached up—as if the dead spell on them fell away—and tore their pointed branches off with gnarled root fingers. The tree army shot their weapons at Hekate and her men, the jagged daggers hitting their mark again and again as the soldiers dropped on the field, leaving their horses to run off.

But Hekate and her few remaining men kept coming, out of the way of the tree soldiers. The weapons of the woods fell short and tree arms, once buried in the ground, froze in the air.

And then a figure on a horse punched through the mist.

He launched through the air, a hero of giant proportions.

Bo Chez!

I'll always come for you, he'd said.

He tore through the fog, speeding up from behind our enemy. And hope shot through me as if I had been pierced by Leandro's arrow.

Hekate saw him and yelled to her men, the ten or so soldiers left to fight. They turned in an arc, heading right for Bo Chez.

Leandro reined his horse in. "Quick," he said to me. "Get off and into the gate."

"No!"

"It's not your day to die a hero." And he left me no choice as he dumped me on the ground.

"Your Majesty." Leandro held out the reins of the other horse to him, and the king mounted it in one swoop.

"Take these." Sam ran over and handed his and Charlie's vapes to them. They grabbed them and, together, cantered off after Hekate.

"Send the kids home," Leandro yelled back at me. "You too."

"Not without Bo Chez!" My words faded away as horses stampeded the meadow.

Leandro circled around to join Bo Chez, and Hekate and her men raced after him, away from us.

I ran to my friends. Fear filled Finn's face, his freckles jumping up and down as he chewed on the inside of his cheek.

"Did the other kids get through?" I said.

Sam nodded weakly, and his pinched face told me how much older and tired he'd become. By now the Moria plant's magic had to be wearing off, and

Leandro didn't have any more leaves. Sam's time was running out. So was all of ours.

"Hurry!" Sam directed the remaining kids under the gate. I pressed my fingers to the column next to him, wanting to soak up its legendary power as it hummed with electricity. Its carvings flowed in and out of one another as if they were gathering up the gate's energy to zap everyone home. Time to use it for good instead of evil. The kids looked at me with wide eyes, scared and hopeful all at once.

"We're almost at max capacity," Sam said, peering at the Lightning Gate key he'd pushed into the gate like a puzzle piece. He studied the scroll and pressed a series of jeweled squares on the golden box that lit up and flashed. "There's room for only two more on this trip."

"Charlie, get out of here." It took all the energy I had left to push him under the gate.

"Wait!" He reached in his pocket. "Sam, here, the bag." Sam hesitated, but I grabbed it for him. "I'm glad I followed you, Joshua!"

"Stay cool, Charlie," I said. We once thought we'd never leave this place, and now goodbye came so fast. He'd see his brother again.

"You're the cool one, Joshua." And we smiled at each other. "*Au revoir, mes amies*!" He shoved a piece of bark in my hand, then ran into the crowd of kids. "That's goodbye—"

"For now, until—"

"We meet again, my friends!" Then he disappeared in the crowd.

I opened my hand to see Charlie's final picture, roughly drawn with the charcoal from a burnt stick. On it, two kids painted on easels next to each other by a creek. One tall. One short. And they were smiling at each other. It was signed. *Joshua and Charlie went home.*

Awesome.

I slid the bark into my pocket, careful not to smudge it, and turned to Finn. "We'll meet back at my house, okay?" I pushed him forward.

He smiled bravely, but his lip wobbled. What if they all got blown to bits instead of saved? He punched my arm weakly and said, "Ham and cheese." And I knew it would be okay. He ran into the gate.

"That's it," Sam said, and punched a final button on the gate key. "The default setting. To return them from where they each last came."

Then the lights on the key box died.

A quick glance to the meadow showed Bo Chez and Leandro dodging vape fire. But for how much longer?

Sam's fingers shook as he tried another combination on the key. It wouldn't light up again. The fight grew closer. "Hurry, Sam. Hurry!" I croaked out, my throat dry from racing breaths that barreled up my throat.

"I'm trying! I thought I had it, but now it won't work!"

The ground trembled. A rumble of hooves echoed close.

"Sam, can't you fire the gate's weapons?"

He shook his head, studying the scroll and working the panel furiously. "Only kings have the secret code to fire Lightning Gate power."

Just our luck. The king was fighting for his life right now, and he barely missed Hekate's fingers of death. I pulled out the orb and prayed it wouldn't hit Leandro, Bo Chez, or the king as I threw it at the mass heading our way. *Blast!*

Horses fell. Screams filled the air. Sam frantically worked at the key in the Lightning Gate. The orb came back to me. I threw it again and again. No hesitation now.

The kids cried for help, hiding behind me. "Hurry, Sam!"

He pulled out the gate key and pushed it back in.

"It's jammed!" He took the key out and tried it again.

Fire bolts spun like spears before us. Vapes lashed out with their deadly tongues. Arrows rained down.

"Got it!" He cried.

I turned my head to see, barely dodging vape fire. The key's squares flashed with brilliant color. The gate glowed, and a golden sheen moved through it like liquid. Its glimmer grew so bright it was like the sun itself. The kids standing underneath it shimmered. White light exploded from the gate. The air sizzled, and the kids vanished.

The last thing I saw was Charlie's head above everyone else's, and Finn's freckles.

Chapter Forty-One

I pulled Sam down behind the Lightning Gate. He gripped the bag that was his one hope.

It had grown too murky now to see well enough to throw the orb, and I could barely make out Leandro's cloak. Vape smoke surged with the mist like steam from an angry brew. The king fired his vape at his own soldiers, now loyal to Hekate.

Bo Chez raised up his arms and threw them out with a grand sweep. A gray ball burst from his hands. It exploded over Hekate and her men, trapping them in a giant storm. Bo Chez then raced on his horse around the massive ball tethered to him, dragging it along. The dust had cleared enough to see the soldiers inside. They smashed into the walls of the storm ball to bust through it, their horses dashing about in panic, but none could break free.

"To The Great Beyond!" Bo Chez yelled, and took

off into the woods.

"Wait, Bo Chez!" *Don't leave me again! I want to go with you*!

But he was gone and the ball he dragged rolled around the trees, stretching like a slingshot between the narrow spaces and then forming a ball again in the open. It soon disappeared into the woods. Leandro turned back toward us, the enemy gone, when Hekate and the Child Collector appeared behind him through the trees. They had broken free somehow from Bo Chez's storm! And what had happened to King Apollo?

"Leandro, watch out," Sam and I yelled at the same time. Hekate and the Child Collector bashed into Leandro's horse. He almost fell, but gained his balance and turned on them, just missing Hekate's fire power. He aimed his vape at the Child Collector, who scowled at him and raised his vape, too. *Zap. Zap.* They missed each other!

The Child Collector saw me hiding behind the gate and turned his horse my way, his red face forever scorched in my mind. I swore he would never hurt anyone again.

He galloped faster, and as he raced closer, it felt like Hekate's entire cavalry of horses thundered through my chest. My legs shook, but I willed them steady.

Yeah, just you and me.

The trees around the field waved their arms, and the mist swirled faster as if they both urged me to take down this monster.

"You and your grandfather stole my rightful life,"

the Child Collector shouted at me. "You're going down, Reeker. Payback!"

Power surged through me.

Time to stop the Child Collector before he killed again.

This monster had killed my mother, stolen Finn, then me, and profited from our enslavement. If it weren't for him, I would have known my mother.

He would not take Leandro too.

I didn't understand all that had happened, but Leandro had sacrificed himself to save us—and he was doing so again.

This would end here and now.

Closer and closer the Child Collector got. His horse snorted as he kicked it on.

His one eye burned bright from his scarred flesh. He rushed at me, pulling his horse up fast.

I stepped out from behind the Lightning Gate and flung the orb with all my might as he leapt for me.

The Child Collector's mouth hung open, and it was the last I saw of his frightening face before the orb entered his mouth. *Boom!* He disappeared in a flash, except for his cloak, which floated to the ground. His horse ran off. The orb landed back in my hand. Dizziness flooded me. I swayed and let out a huge breath.

Payback.

"No!" Hekate's wail echoed around the battle zone. Sam and I backed up as she galloped toward us, but it was her brother's cloak she headed for, nearly falling off her horse to pick it up. She rubbed it across her cheek, her shoulders shaking. "Cronag, my Cronag." Her tears wet the only thing left of him. "You'll never get that new body now."

Stunned at her sudden show of emotion, Sam and I were frozen, but Leandro wasn't. He'd reached her, firing his vape at the witch. She stumbled twice, a blast nicking her side, then hauled herself up on her horse, cloak in hand. She and Leandro circled one another like boxers in a ring as their horses tore up the ground, their breaths beating the air in angry chuffs.

Leandro shot at her again. This time her horse sprung away just in time. Then, in a split second, she threw her hand up in the air. Blue light from her fingertips struck Leandro in the chest. He fell off his horse and was still.

So still.

Leandro, get up, please. But he didn't.

Hekate reeled her horse around and headed to the Lightning Gate.

Sam pulled me back as Hekate grew closer, and her hair whipped through the air like angry snakes. My orb was ready in hand. Could I hit her or would she grab the orb again, unhurt?

And still Leandro didn't get up.

Sam pushed my hand down and stepped forward.

"Traitorous Prince!" Tears streaked her pale face in blotchy patches. She raised her hand at me as she closed the gap between us. "And *you*, Oracle or not, you're dead. You killed my family. Now I'll kill you!"

Sam quickly stepped to Hekate's other side as she reached us and grabbed the reins of her horse. "You won't kill my friend." And he flung the open bag. A white cloud *poofed* in the air, then fell on her.

And he said, in a voice louder, stronger, and more confident than I'd ever heard him use, "Ashes to dust, is what's left of me. Unless, to live, I pass this to thee. Then ashes to dust now you will be."

A terrible screech exploded from Hekate. Her horse stopped in its tracks and through the air she sailed. She landed face down, clutching her brother's cloak, as still as Leandro.

Sam and I crept up on the fallen witch. Her green robe and hair fanned out over the ground. A faint groan grew deep inside her into a rumbling bawl. She pushed herself up, thrashing her head about, her hands and face as shriveled as Sam's had been. Only then did I think to check out Sam. He was a kid again! He looked at his hands and arms in amazement.

The curse had passed.

"Cronag, I'll find a way. Bring you back," she croaked as she transformed into an ancient hag. Wrinkles crisscrossed her face. She pulled at her hair and it fell out in white clumps. Sam and I stepped back as Hekate clawed her face. "My beauty," she hissed, pointing at us, but her gnarled fingertips no longer sparked. A cloud burst from her mouth, and her sickening rose scent wafted over me, then disappeared. She moaned and sank into her quilted grave.

"No one owns me. Can you hear me? *Can*

you?" Sam shouted at the wadded up pile of green shuddering on the ground.

"I'll. Be. Back," the lump whispered, and then was still.

Chapter Forty-Two

We ran to Leandro's side.

Sam dropped down beside me. Leandro's long hair spread out around him. His hand clutched at his dagger, unmoving, and a gash on his forehead blazed against his pale skin. He looked so different with his eyes closed—like an ordinary dad in some movie, asleep on a Sunday morning before his kids tackled him and woke him up. I slid my hand down the scar that cut across his face, then put my finger on the large hole where Hekate had struck him in the chest. His heart was beating! "Sam, he's alive!"

Quickly, I shoved aside Leandro's cloak and grabbed his worn satchel, desperate that he be wrong about the Moria leaves, and pulled out a few glow sticks, his journal, and his son's bow, wishing all the while he was awake and angry at me for going through it. I slipped my hand into his bag and ran my fingers around inside.

Nothing. This couldn't be happening!

"Joshua, you've done what you could." Sam touched my arm. "I know it's hard to lose a friend—"

"No!" I had no description for what Leandro meant to me, but it was more than friendship. I looked up to him, learned from him, needed to draw from his hope that he'd one day reunite with his wife and child—I needed that as much as I had needed to find Finn and return home. "He's got to live."

What good was having powers if you couldn't save someone? I turned the satchel inside out and shook it. Still nothing, not one piece of a leaf. Panic growing, I felt around the seams for anything that might cling there—and my finger snagged on a rotted thread. I worked open the hole with my thumb and there, in the seam, hid two more leaves.

My trembling fingers pulled them out, crushed them, and pushed them through the hole of Leandro's shirt. Taking a deep breath, I pressed them hard into his wound, trying not to faint from the blood oozing around my fingers. *Live, Leandro, live!*

"It's not your day to die a hero," I told him as I searched the sky for answers, but found none. The branches of the trees fell limp again and the fog stood still, holding its breath as we waited. I lay my face on Leandro's chest, desperate for other signs of hope and breathed in his pungent smell of earth and leather … and life.

"Wake up," I whispered. "By the arrow of Artemis, wake up!"

Silence. Mist wet my cheeks. I kept my eyes closed for a long while. Sam tugged at my shirt, but I pushed him away. And then a heavy hand grazed my head.

"I wasn't sleeping."

My eyes flew open. Leandro was staring at me. I threw my arms across him and hugged him hard. He moaned in pain and I got off him, forgetting he likely had other injuries.

"Did you heal me?" he said.

"No, I found some Moria leaves in your bag."

"I thought it was all gone."

"A few pieces were hidden," I said.

"Maybe it was a combination." He looked at me with a raised eyebrow.

"So, do you trust me now?" I managed a laugh.

But he didn't laugh with me, his face was serious. "You had my trust before saving my life. But I almost failed to save you from Hekate."

"We saved each other, Leandro."

He squeezed my hand twice before letting go.

"And Hekate's dead," I said.

"Even the trees came to our aid," Sam said.

"Hekate must have cursed the trees here long ago, and now her power, and spell, is gone. I've heard stories of how these trees were once defenders of good."

"Look," I said, pointing. Green shoots poked out from the tree branches.

"Coming back to life indeed." Sam's eyes were shining.

"Now it won't look like winter here all the time," I said.

"And the mist is lifting," Sam cried, pointing around us. It was true! The lavender sky painted itself lighter and the blue sun shone bright for the first time as the fog uncurled from around the trees and slowly receded.

"Perhaps the light will finally reach our land with Hekate gone," Sam said, a rare smile on his face, and he looked like a regular kid for once. "Our land has been cursed a long, long time."

"Indeed," Leandro said. "Funny how one young mortal helped bring that about." Our eyes locked for a long moment. I didn't know what brought an end to the mist, or the spell the trees had been under, but couldn't deny the light that burst from the sky everywhere.

"Sol," Sam said in a voice full of wonder, lifting his hands to the sun, then together we helped Leandro up. He looked around. "What about the Child Collector?"

"The Child Collector ate the orb," I said. "I blasted him into nothing."

"Good," Leandro said. "Better that there's nothing left of that vile man. And Hekate is dead for sure?"

I pointed at her lumpy robe and her brother's cloak, quickly explaining what happened.

"The old ones go quickly with a curse," Leandro said. "She must have been very old."

"But she looked young, for a grownup," I said.

"Immortality will do that. And evil spells." Leandro pressed his lips in a fine line.

"She said she'll be back."

"Could be. There are tales of immortal Ancient Ones coming back from the dead, especially if their power is very strong. But that's a fight for another day." Leandro smiled. "It's good to see you back, Sam. You and Joshua, the great smiters of evil."

Whatever a smiter was, it sure sounded good to me.

"What happened with you and Bo Chez?" I said. "I thought you both died in that crash, and then you showed up with him as your prisoner."

Sam seemed confused, so I quickly filled him in on all that happened while he had been sending kids home through the Lightning Gate and fighting off bad guys.

"I bruised some ribs when we went down." Leandro winced, holding his side. "We took Hekate's soldier unaware, got him to confess where she was headed, and after knocking him out and stashing my weapons, we rode to find you at the armory."

"What about Bo Chez?" I said.

"He hit a tree so hard he should have died."

"Why didn't he?"

Leandro just looked at me, as if deciding what to tell me. "I knew what he was then."

"What is he?" I said, the blood throbbing in my ears.

"He carries the great name of Patrok, a hero of the Trojan war. And he is what you had hoped for, Joshua," Leandro said solemnly.

"What do you mean?"

Leandro put a hand on my arm as if to prepare me, the throb in my ears pounding faster alongside the pulse from his fingertips.

"Your grandfather is an immortal Ancient One. He's been around since the early days, right after the Olympians left Mount Olympus for good."

"Like Hekate?" I could barely find my voice, and Sam's eyes widened. *That's why she'd said she'd seen Bo Chez before!*

"Yes, but a *good* immortal Ancient One," Leandro said.

"He can't die?"

"A curse can kill him, but there are ways to come back."

"Like Hekate could," I said.

"Yes, but he told me he's thwarted her before on Nostos as a young man, and he'll do it again."

It all started to make sense now. "And you and Bo Chez tricked Hekate into believing you were undercover and he was your prisoner so you could rescue me?"

Leandro nodded. If my world had turned upside down before, it did again. Bo Chez had lived for thousands of years. He could live for thousands more. It was hard to grasp, that like the infinite space of the universe, my grandfather was infinite too.

"And Hekate's brother was immortal too?"

Sam shook his head. "Not exactly. She's been spinning ancient magic and using the bodies of others for centuries to keep his soul alive."

"So what happens now that he's vaporized?" I looked to both of them for answers.

"Let's hope his soul is gone now that it has no body to attach to," Leandro said, and Sam nodded.

"I don't understand though. If Bo Chez is immortal, why didn't he stay young like Hekate?"

"He told me he lost his power of immortality when he went to Earth," Leandro said. "He began aging there, although at a slower rate than mortals. And it's why Hekate didn't recognize him at first."

"So he'll live forever here but die on Earth?"

"Yes."

So going home would save me, but kill Bo Chez. He would someday die there, like me. But here, he would never die unless a bad curse killed him. He must have really wanted a new life to give up immortality and choose a new world.

Sam cut through my thoughts. "Where's my father—King Apollo?" He jerked his head about.

"I thought I saw him follow Joshua's grandfather." Leandro's energy had already returned to the point that he jumped around. "Over here!"

Sam and I followed him through the grass toward the woods. The disappearing fog barely camouflaged the dead soldiers we ran past, and there, slumped against a tree, sprawled King Apollo. Leandro helped me roll him over. The king bled from a bad cut to his head and gasped for air.

Leandro knelt behind him and put the king's head on his knees. "Joshua, you must have found more

Moria plant … "

"You're only alive because I found the last of it hidden in your bag," I said. "It's all gone."

The king opened his eyes. "Don't guess I'll get my kingdom back now, will I?"

Leandro bowed his head. "If it soothes your soul, sire, Hekate won't be ruling either. Sam killed her."

The king wheezed. "Good."

Sam knelt by his side. "I'm sorry about all this, Father."

"Not your fault, my boy. If I'd treated you better—if I'd treated everyone better—it never would have come to this. I should have worked to find a better energy solution for the Lost Realm."

"We can now. It's never too late for a new beginning," Sam said, and reached his hand out. He hesitated, then placed it on the king's chest, and the king placed his own hand over it.

"I really did love your mother, Sam."

"I know," Sam whispered.

"But I closed my heart to her, and all our people. I'm so sorry." A fat tear rolled down the king's cheek.

"Your heart is open now, Father."

The king touched Sam's face, and then his arm fell to his side.

Leandro folded his cloak and placed it beneath the king's head. "Sire, I want you to know, I'll travel across Nostos to find help for the Lost Realm."

"Not if there's a warrant out for your arrest." The king's breath came in long gasps. "Need to pardon you." He coughed a horrible sound like wet paper being crushed in his lungs. "Paper ... my handwriting can be verified. With my ... " He turned to Sam. "My son as witness, it will be good throughout Nostos."

Leandro was already pulling paper and pen from a buckled pocket on the front of his satchel. The king wrote for a minute with a shaky hand, then handed the sheet to Leandro. "I've recommended you for higher service to Queen Artemis as well." He turned to Sam. "Here, Son, take this." He removed his pinkie ring. "You've proved yourself to lead. I choose you to take my place. Band with Leandro to help you. All shall now know that you can act on my behalf to lead the Lost Realm. You've lived with mortals. You'll be the most sympathetic to their plight. Carry on the legacy I never could ... "

Sam bent over and took the ring, pushing it down onto his thumb. "I will, Father."

"One more thing you must do."

Sam leaned in closer.

"Go to Earth. Find your mother. Tell her ... tell her I'm sorry."

The king closed his eyes and didn't move again. Sam put his head on the chest of his king, his father. Leandro and I were quiet as Sam said goodbye. We then covered the king with branches.

"There's nothing more we can do here. Let's go get your grandfather, Joshua," Leandro finally said. Sam wiped his face and nodded. My sadness for him mixed with my own, fearful Bo Chez had suffered the same fate. I pushed that thought away as Leandro and I called to the kernitians, in the hope they would return to transport us again. They did.

As we flew up to the treetops in the growing light toward The Great Beyond, the king's body grew smaller and smaller. Then, with a drift of the fading mist, he disappeared.

Chapter Forty-Three

"There," Leandro pointed below. A man on a horse raced between the trees. Bo Chez! We zoomed down, yelling at him to stop. Just seeing him made the knots in my chest unravel, and I practically fell off my kernitian to get to him. He dismounted and hugged me tight, his thick arms gripping me, alive and magical as ever.

"I don't blame you for my mother dying, Bo Chez." My heart thumped inside me with gladness that he was okay, and that I had the chance to take back those words. I swore I would make it up to Bo Chez for the rest of my life, if not his.

"I know," he said softly.

"I was just so angry that the Child Collector killed her."

Then it hit me. Family wasn't made by blood—it was made by love. And love was stronger than fear.

Bo Chez might not be my true blood, but we were connected to this world, and that connected us, stronger than ever.

"Leandro told me everything," I said.

"So now you understand." His eyes pierced me in a new way, as if I had become an equal in his adventures and now must pass the final test.

I slowly nodded. "But, you've really been around forever?"

Then Bo Chez laughed. His face cracked open, and he once again became my grandfather. "Not forever, but some time, yes."

"You said you'd always come for me."

"And I will."

And that was all I needed to make sense of, for now.

"Good to have you back with us, Patrok," Leandro said, breaking the silence with my grandfather's real name, reminding me of the true hero he had become to all of us.

"So, what did you do with the army, Bo Chez?" I said.

"Did you send them into The Great Beyond?" Sam wanted to know.

"On the way to The Edge, they had a change of heart. One minute they were angry warriors and the next they were simple men, begging for their lives. So, I let them go and they ran off."

"Hekate is dead," Sam said, dismounting from his kernitian. "For now, anyway. I gave her my Old World Curse."

Bo Chez studied Sam for a few moments. "You must be Sam, then."

Sam nodded.

"That would explain it—Hekate probably enchanted the soldiers, and her power died with her, perhaps the fog as well that she most likely created. And now the sky grows lighter. The sun is finally reaching the Lost Realm for the first time. Let's hope she doesn't find magic to come back." Bo Chez tilted his head. "But why the long face, Sam? We've destroyed an enemy, and your youth has been restored—"

"My father ... "

"The king is dead," I filled in, when it looked as if Sam couldn't continue speaking.

Bo Chez put a hand on Sam's shoulder. "I'm very sorry for your loss, Sam."

I now kind of understood how confusing family love could be. When it came to my own family, love and anger had a pretty rickety fence between them.

"And—" I didn't think the words would come, but the thrill of revenge brought them out. "And I blasted the Child Collector."

Bo Chez blew out a big breath. "Are you okay, Joshua?"

I nodded, then shook my head, not knowing how to feel about it. But I'd erased the Child Collector, and his smell, forever. No more nightmares.

"Taking a man's life—even an evil man's—is never easy, even for an old warrior like me. Nostos is a better place without him. Now it would seem there's only one thing left to do."

"What's that, Bo Chez?"

He cocked his head at me, his jagged hair shining with the last of the mist. He might be from another world with magical powers, but—hey, so was I.

He put his thick arms around me and hugged me tight. "Why, we go home, Joshua." Finn might have a whole family to share, but Bo Chez and I shared a whole world.

"Finn's already home." I couldn't stop smiling now. "And Sam. Can he come home with us? We'll help him find his mother."

Bo Chez nodded and took Sam into our hug.

Then Sam and Leandro flew back to the Lightning Gate while Bo Chez and I galloped back on his horse through the woods no longer shrouded in mist. White cloud patches painted over the purple the sky, like an artist creating a new picture on an old, dingy canvas. Even the dead trees looked alive to me now, and they moved their branches apart to welcome our passage. Maybe Hekate's death did give them new life.

We finally stood before the Lightning Gate, where all that remained of Hekate and her brother was a green robe and a cloak. Bo Chez kicked them to make sure they were empty. A spark flashed and, just like that, they burst into flames. We watched them burn and crumble into ash.

My excitement over them being gone faded to waves of exhaustion. "I just want be a kid again."

"And you shall, Joshua," Leandro said. "But I have

the feeling you'll be back. For now, the Lost Realm folk must figure out their own problems."

"But they fixed their problems before by doing bad things," I said.

"This time they'll do good things to survive. I'll make sure," Leandro said.

"And so will I," Sam said.

"Perhaps we'll call on you for help another time," Leandro said.

"But not now." Bo Chez put a protective arm around my shoulder, and I had the feeling Leandro was right—this would not be my last Nostos adventure.

"How will you find me, Leandro?" I said. "We move a lot."

"Not anymore, Joshua," Bo Chez said, and gave Leandro our address.

"Really?" I said.

"Really."

We all stood there, safe for the first time in days. And the word *home* floated in my head like a gift waiting to be unwrapped. A gift that held everything now.

"Time for me to go, too," Leandro finally said.

It hit me hard. Leandro was *actually leaving* us? After all we'd been through?

I looked into his eyes, that stormy mix of color, not wanting to forget him. "Which land are you going to?"

He placed his hands on his hips and thrust his chin upward, his long roped hair swaying with the thickest white streak like a lifeline. "To the Arrow Realm. It's my land, and Artemis may be the best leader for me to appeal to for finding a new source of power for the Lost Realm—and to stop stealing mortal children for Nostos. Perhaps she'll consider looking to her own people for answers and appeal to Zeus to change all of our world."

Sam pushed the key into the gate and unfurled the scroll of codes. He then punched in the combination that would connect with the Arrow Realm.

When all was set, Leandro looked at us one by one, and my joy of going home fizzled at the thought that I might never see him again. He grasped both my forearms. A warrior's goodbye. I gripped him back, and looked up to him one last time.

"Young Joshua, I don't think this is your final victory. You have other battles to win—on Earth or here."

I cleared my throat. "They were wrong about you. You're not a broken arrow."

He smiled at that, his eyes sparkling in the brightening sun. "Perhaps. Marks on the outside do not always make the man on the inside. Remember to believe in yourself and you will have the power to be whatever destiny drives you to be."

"I'll never see you again." I didn't want to believe my words. Our connection had grown fierce.

"Yes you will." Leandro grasped my arms harder, then let go and put a fist to his chest. "I feel it." From his satchel he pulled out the small bow he had made and handed it to me.

"But this is for your son." I held it tight in my hands. "I want you to have it."

Thank you didn't begin to cover it, but that's all I could mumble.

"If I ever find my son, he will have outgrown it anyway."

"Maybe he is the Oracle waiting to happen, Leandro."

"Or maybe you are after all. Maybe there is more to the myth than we know."

No one spoke. The idea of being the Oracle twisted uncomfortably up inside me.

Leandro turned and shook hands with Bo Chez and Sam, then walked into the Lightning Gate. It was a quiet moment with just us here, the sounds of battle gone, and a silent bronze giant that stood as a doorway between realms—and worlds.

"Wait, Leandro," I said. "We have your gate key. How will you travel between lands to keep looking for your family and then take them to Earth?"

"I won't need it to travel undercover now. I'm a pardoned man." He drew out King Apollo's letter. "Although, I'll keep my traveling belt, just in case. And I now have hope that our world can change in time. Perhaps we can make a life here. Or perhaps someday we will be free to go to Earth if we choose." He then nodded at Sam who pushed the key into the gate. The ancient metal glowed, and a golden halo radiated around Leandro.

I pulled out the orb, pressed it to my chest, and

then held it up to him in goodbye. He lifted his hand, and with a flash of light was gone.

I slid the orb into my pocket with little enthusiasm for our own journey home, and looked over at Sam. He gave me that same little knowing smile he'd given me when first holding that clipboard. And now he'd be like a brother to me for a while, back on Earth, where we would help him find his mother. A new adventure was about to unfold.

I tapped Sam on the back. "Ready for Earth?" He hesitated, then punched in the code, placed the key in its place, and accompanied us into the Lightning Gate.

But before heading under its thick columns I needed to read its inscription aloud, to defy it. "Honor the fire of Zeus that sparks your journey. Adversity breeds true power. Bow to the gods."

"You can read Greek?" Sam said with wide eyes.

Greek, huh. "Doesn't surprise me in this place," I half-joked.

"Me either, especially with your evident power here," Bo Chez said. "But no more bowing to the gods now, Joshua."

Sam nodded in agreement. Then I stepped into the powerful machine beside him to go home.

I sucked in a whiff of electric fire. Sparks started to fly around my belly. The lightning filled me up with strength, not fear.

That's when something unexpected happened.

Sam pulled out the key and stepped back from the gate.

"Light of Sol go with you, my friends," he said.

"What?" I looked at Bo Chez and back at Sam. The sparks in my belly traveled out into my arms and buzzed through my hands, tugging on my nerves. "Sam, your mother. We can find her now. You can find a way back later."

"Perhaps." He fingered the royal ring on his thumb. "But my people here need me right now even more than I need a lost mother. That's for certain. This is my home. I can help the people of the Lost Realm find a better energy solution and lead them into a better life."

Sam may have looked like a kid again, but as he stood with his feet wide apart, his chest out, and his head held high he looked wise, courageous, and every bit a king. His mother was lost to him, his father now dead, and he'd been an outcast in his own family, but he was still willing to sacrifice to make a difference beyond his own needs. I had to follow my quest, now he chose his. I couldn't argue with him. I wanted a brother, but he had a whole kingdom to save.

"Wherever you come from, Joshua, know this: you *are* a true light bringer," Sam said in a strong voice. "Your getting stolen away to our world gave us the light of hope, the strongest light of all."

The sky broke open, covering us in a jeweled violet, pushing the dark away. I blinked from the brightness and raised my hand. "Light of Sol go with you, too."

And with that, Sam pushed the key back into the gate.

Chapter Forty-Four

Light exploded everywhere, and Bo Chez held my hand so tight it hurt. The wind roared and lightning whipped around us in the black tunnel. We shot through the darkness, faster and faster. Then Finn stood before us in the attic in a T-shirt and jeans again. A smile spread across his freckled face.

It was over. We were home. We were alive.

Finn piled on me in one leap. "Joshua! That was like a minute. I just had time to change."

"But it's been longer than that since we last saw you." I peeked out the window. The rain had stopped. The yellow sun shone bright from a clear, pale blue sky, and the creek roared past the house, full from the recent rain.

Finn plucked at Leandro's bow, and I placed it on a nearby chair. It looked so out of place in our world. Then Finn ran to the attic stairs. "Where's Sam?"

"He decided to stay," I said.

He nodded as if he understood.

Bo Chez put his watch to his ear and shook it. "If this thing still works, just the night has passed. It's morning now."

"But we've been gone for days," I said.

"Different world, different time," Bo Chez said.

"And now we have our own time again," I said.

"So let's make the most of it, boys."

Finn and I nodded at each other. I felt in my back pocket for my mother's photo. We had both been stolen away to the Lost Realm and traveled back home again. I remembered Sam's flute and drew it out, put it to my lips, and blew. A horrible squeal burst out and a bird squawked outside my window in response. I had no idea what it said. It was the end of musical powers and malumpus-tongue for me back on Earth. About time.

I looked down at the dark sun brand on my arm and tried to once again read the words encircling it. The Greek letters made no sense to me now, but it reminded me to appreciate all the freedoms in my life. More permanent were the brands on my heart. Leandro. Sam. Charlie. I wondered if I'd meet any of them again.

Deep tiredness sank in, but more than a nap, I was desperate to be normal again.

"Still wanna play hide-n-seek, Finn?" I said.

He laughed. "Nah. How about we go outside and build our fort?"

"Can we?" I tugged on Bo Chez's shirt.

He acted like we'd insulted him. "What, you don't want to hear one of my stories instead?"

"Bo Chez, we've *lived* the story."

"Then get out of here before it starts raining again." He put his hands on his hips. "I'll make us all some pancakes and ice cream sodas. Then we all need hot showers. And a good long sleep. Want to stay another night, Finn?"

"As long as we don't go anywhere!" And with that, Finn took off down the stairs. "Race ya to the yard!"

But I still had one thing left to do. I pulled the lightning orb out of my pocket and handed it to Bo Chez. He put his big hand around it. We held it together, our connection between worlds and history. The orb's blue glowed between our fingers, then dimmed, but I knew what kind of power lay hidden within it—and within me. Knowing it would still be there whenever I needed it, I let go.

I took off down the attic stairs, after Finn, and burst into the yard. Something made me stop and turn back to look up at the attic window. Bo Chez stood there, arms crossed, looking down at us through the shattered glass. Watching over me.

He broke into a grin. I waved at him and dashed after Finn under the safe, sunny sky.

The lightning was gone. For now.

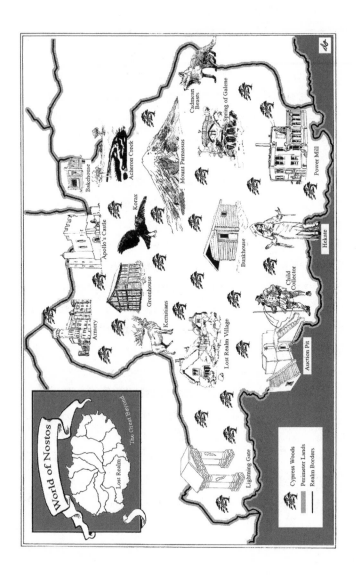

ACKNOWLEDGEMENTS

So many wonderful and supportive people helped get this book published. Kathryn Craft, my dear friend and editor, who guided me in shaping this tale – and who helped me shape myself as an author. My understanding husband Michael, the greatest provider of alone time there is! My first reader and cosmic sister, Lisa Green, who inspired me to find the power in the details. So many more moved this book along the road to publication including the dedicated staff of Month9Books, my literary agent, Bill Contardi, who took a chance on a new author, and my wonderful Weggie Writers group of gals who trudged alongside me as this book came to life. And to the person who began this book, the real Joshua Cooper Galanti. I wrote this for you. May you never grow too old for bedtime stories and may you always seek just one more adventure.

DONNA GALANTI

Donna Galanti wanted to be a writer ever since she wrote a murder mystery screenplay at seven and acted it out with the neighborhood kids. She attended an English school housed in a magical castle, where her wild imagination was held back only by her itchy uniform (bowler hat and tie included!). There she fell in love with the worlds of C.S. Lewis and Roald Dahl, and wrote her first fantasy about Dodo birds, wizards, and a flying ship (and has been writing fantasy ever since). She's lived in other exotic locations, including her family-owned campground in New Hampshire and in Hawaii where she served as a U.S. Navy photographer. She now lives with her family and two crazy cats in an old farmhouse and dreams of returning one day to a castle. Donna is the author of the JOSHUA AND THE LIGHTNING ROAD series (Month9Books). Visit her at:

Website:
http://donnagalanti.com/

Facebook:
https://www.facebook.com/DonnaGalantiAuthor

Twitter:
https://twitter.com/DonnaGalanti

Pinterest:
http://www.pinterest.com/donnagalanti/

GoodReads:
https://www.goodreads.com/author/show/5767306.
Donna_Galanti

Other MONTH9BOOKS and TANTRUM
BOOKS titles you might like:

THE THREE THORNS
KING OF THE MUTANTS
GABRIEL STONE AND THE WRATH OF THE
SOLARIANS
TRACY TAM: SANTA COMMAND

THE
BROTHERHOOD
AND THE
SHIELD
THE THREE THORNS
MICHAEL GIBNEY

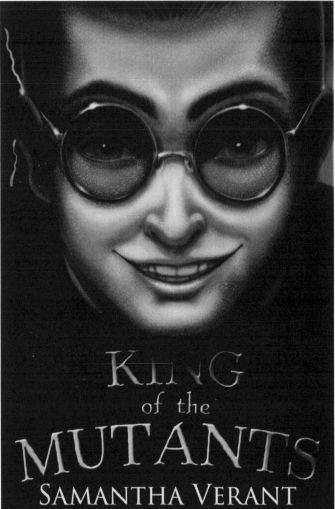

KING
of the
MUTANTS
SAMANTHA VERANT

DEAD JED

DAWN OF THE JED

SCOTT CRAVEN

· 2 ·

TRACY TAM
SANTA COMMAND

KRYSTALYN DROWN

GABRIEL STONE
· AND ·
THE WRATH OF THE SOLARIANS

SHANNON DUFFY